...Don'

I kept t wanting to see what he had done to my soon as my bedroom door was shut behind me I looked down to find there was now a tattoo where he had grabbed me. Three V's, their points meeting in the center, expanding out to form an almost circular pattern with smaller lines swirling around the letters almost like vines. I traced the patterns with the finger of my other hand and a tingle of warmth oozed from the spot.

"Fuck," I whisper, dropping my towel and grabbing a pair of jeans. I now wore the mark of a demon, and I hadn't even had breakfast yet.

I finished dressing and picked up my cell phone, letting it rest in my hand while I contemplated dialing the police. How would I even explain the situation? *Oh, this man I just had a dream about is in my apartment. I don't know who he is but I'm pretty sure he's a demon... No, he hasn't threatened me, he wants to have tea!* I stifle a laugh and stuff the phone down into my pocket. "Jesus Christ," I mutter, "I'm in deep shit."

Conquered

Jezka Brash

© 2015 Jezka Brash

ISBN-13: 978-1515380290

ISBN-10: 1515380297

Cover designed by Jezka Brash

Dedicated to Aunt Carole and Julie Bug

*You two always encouraged me to follow my
dreams before I could even walk.
I wouldn't be the woman I was today without your
love and support.
I know you are looking down on me with a smile
right now at all that I've achieved.
I love you both.*

Conquered

Chapter One

** Jacki **

I woke in a pool of sweat gasping for breath as tears were streaming down my face. My heart was racing and never before had a dream left me so terrified. I lay there a few moments trying to steady my breathing before getting up to take a shower. I let the steam fill the bathroom before stepping in and letting the hot water wash away each vivid detail.

I had glanced out the window to watch the traffic pass by underneath me. All I could see for miles was highway and suddenly all kinds of wrecks were happening. There was a smaller blue sports car weaving in and out of oncoming traffic. The highway was busy and cars were spinning out of control to avoid hitting this madman. I thought at first that it was some sort of police chase, yet no one seemed to be following the car. I couldn't look away as the little blue vehicle found its target.

A white Cadillac barely managed to swerve their car enough to avoid getting hit head on, but it was enough of a tail end hit to send both cars spinning out of control into the ditch below my window. Glass shattered, and smoke poured from both cars as two large men jumped out of the Caddy. Every inch of their bodies seemed to bulge with muscle, their skin was covered in tattoos and their heads were shaven bald to look like stereotypical club bouncers.   They had guns and they looked pissed.

I pulled out my phone to try and ring the police, but I was shaking so badly that it dropped to the ground and shattered to pieces.   The man in the blue car finally appeared, rolling out of his door while laughing hysterically. He looked normal enough if it had been other circumstances. Clean cut and tall with just a hint of a summer's tan splashed across his skin. He had short brown hair and was dressed in tan cargo shorts with a blood splattered white t-shirt.   It seemed as if this hadn't been his first adventure of the day.

Time seemed to slow down as he pulled a gun from the car and fired at the two other men before they could react. He got one in the leg, and I screamed and fell to my knees in horror as I knew what was about to happen.

The lunatic turned his head towards me, and I could swear that he saw me through the tinted windows as he fired the gun.   My screams died in my throat as the glass in front of me shattered, leaving nothing but empty space between the fight and myself.   His eyes focused on mine, and I swore I saw them flare red as he mouthed the words, "Pay attention!"   His own attention snapped back to the two men as a bullet hit his shoulder, and he began laughing again.

I started crying; I couldn't help it. My entire body convulsed into sobs as one of the men reached him, the other a few steps behind due to his shot leg. The second man immediately fired a shot into each of the mad man's kneecaps, and then the other man started beating his face in with the other end of his gun.

The highway was full of carnage from all the car wrecks caused by the man, making it near impossible for police to get through the backed up highway. It seemed the man had planned this well and I doubted it was coincidence as my mind whispered the word *Demon...*

Even as his face was broken open and beat raw he still continued to laugh. I screamed again, my screams beyond my control, unable to stop. It seemed to have distracted them for a moment as both big men turned to look at me, but a moment was all he needed.

"You will NEVER win," he screamed at them, pulling another gun from thin air and fired off all the rounds into the two men. The first goon that had previously been shot in the leg took the most of the shots to his chest, and he fell to his knees.

"You son of a fucking bitch, you're gonna wish we fucking killed you sooner." The second goon raised his gun and fired all of his shots at the lunatic and I watched the bullets disintegrate his hand. He walked closer with each shot, kicking the lunatic's gun away before kicking him in the gut several times until he was doubled over spitting up blood.

My screams had stopped, not by choice, but because my throat had become too raw to make noise anymore. The blue car they were standing next to had caught on fire somehow, and suddenly I knew what was going to happen.

The trunk was wide open from the crash, and I could see the gas jug sitting there waiting. Just as I noticed it, it seemed the big man did too. He grabbed the jug and threw it on the ground, and then hauled the crazy man up into the trunk.

As he reached for the gas jug to pour it over the man, the laughter began again. "Stop fuckin laugh'n, you think this is fuckin' funny?" He poured the entire jug of fuel on the man in the trunk, "You ain't gonna be laugh'n in about five minutes, you gonna be fuckin' DEAD."

The man still laughed and I heard him say, "Fuck you!" and then I swear his gaze traveled to me, and he winked at me.

He fucking WINKED. AT. ME.

The car shifted just as an explosion happened, blinding me for a moment as the entire car went up in flames. So did the man that had been standing there. He dropped to the ground, trying to put out the flames, but they wouldn't seem to go out. He was screaming and burning alive, and nothing could help.

More gunshots fired and the man went still, no longer burning alive. The flames died down, seeming disappointed by his death. My eyes frantically searched for whomever had shot him,

4

and then I saw his partner, still barely alive holding the gun.

He rolled over to look at me as sirens were heard in the distance. I was terrified. I had seen the entire thing and I knew he was going to kill me next. He looked at me and I could see the pain and sadness in his eyes. He half smiled at my terror, and I could barely hear him whisper, "Sorry lil mama" before his body fell limp.

I sat there in silence, my body shaking, and my mind in shock.

The fire truck had finally arrived and they raced to put out the dead man on fire on the ground. The police searched the carnage for signs of life, kicking the guns away from the bodies, while medics tried to see if they could save anyone.

They seemed to be ignoring the car on fire, so I started screaming, "There's a man in that car! There's a man in the car! IN THE TRUNK! A MAN!!"

A few people moved to try and put out the car fire, to see if they could find a man, but they shook their heads. A medic came to look me over, and she paused from looking me over to listen to her radio, "There is no one in that car," she said to me. "You're just in shock, you must have seen a lot."

I heard a laugh behind me. It was HIS laugh, the crazy man from the blue car.

I shoved the paramedic away and spun around. There he was, but it couldn't be. He wasn't burnt to a crisp, or beaten bloody. He looked perfectly fine; clean and in a designer suit looking as if he just stepped out of a fashion magazine. He smiled and winked at me again as he put a finger to his mouth in the universal signal for "Shhh."

At that moment, I knew what he was, and before I could even blink at the realization, the demon vanished, and I woke up.

I reached up and turned off the hot water, shocking my body with the ice cold spray of the shower. I needed these images to go away, to fade with the day like all other dreams before, but I had a feeling they would haunt me for a while.

I allowed a few more moments of the cold spray to cover me before I turned it off, grabbed my towel, and crossed my tiny house to the kitchen. I put a kettle of water on the stove to heat before heading back to my room to dress.

"Hopefully there is enough for two," a man's voice spoke from my couch.

I screamed, terrified of my intruder as I tried to run and pull my towel tighter around myself.

He was up and had his hand over my mouth in less than an instant, silencing me. "Shhh," he whispered, and I went quiet. He was the man from my dream, the demon. My eyes swept around wondering if there was anyone else here.

"We're alone. I'm here to make a request of you." His dark brown eyes seared into mine and I saw them flash red. "I'm going to release you, but you will not make a sound. You will get dressed, and then we'll have tea."

I'm losing my mind. I nodded and he took his hands from my mouth and stepped back. I started to walk towards my room, intent on finding a way out, but he grabbed my arm in his hand. He muttered something in a language I didn't recognize and a flare of heat shot through my skin before he released me again.

Don't look at it, don't look at it... I kept telling myself to get to my room, not wanting to see what he had done to my arm. As soon as my bedroom door was shut behind me I looked down to find there was now a tattoo where he had grabbed me. Three V's, their points meeting in the center, expanding out to form an almost circular pattern with smaller lines swirling around the letters almost like vines. I traced the patterns with the finger of my other hand and a tingle of warmth oozed from the spot.

"Fuck," I whisper, dropping my towel and grabbing a pair of jeans. I now wore the mark of a demon, and I hadn't even had breakfast yet.

I finished dressing and picked up my cell phone, letting it rest in my hand while I contemplated dialing the police. How would I even explain the situation? *Oh, this man I just had a dream about is in my apartment. I don't know who he is but I'm pretty sure he's a demon... No, he hasn't threatened me, he wants to have tea!* I stifle a laugh and stuff the phone down into my pocket. "Jesus Christ," I mutter, "I'm in deep shit."

*****

"I need you to find my son." His words were calm as he set the mug of tea down on the table, his eyes once again searing into me and flashing red.

"What?!" I started laughing and had to put my own mug down before I could regain my composure.

"You may find me to be funny Miss Donovan, but I assure you I am quite serious. He is of course half human, and his witch of a mother has hid him from me long enough. You will find him, and then summon me when you are alone with him."

My laughter stopped and I quietly took him in. The red has faded from his dark brown eyes, his jaw was slightly clenched and I wondered how much patience he truly had.

"My dream last night, you were in it…how?"

"To you, it may have seemed a dream, but it was not. I'm not sure how you managed to be there, in the flesh even. There must be witch or demon heritage in your bloodline." He picked his mug back up and took a drink. "What you recall as a dream was entirely real. I noticed you near the window, your energy felt different, so I focused some of my energy on yours." He shifted slightly and crossed one leg over the other making himself quite comfortable on my small sofa. "By adding my energy to yours, it made you visible to the others there, hence why the medics paid you any mind. Once I realized what I had done, I pulled away and you vanished, most likely waking here."

"So, that fucking nightmare I had of you slaughtering those men, you mean to tell me that it was real? Bullshit. I call bullshit. You have to be fucking with my mind." I get up and go to the kitchen, dropping my mug in the sink with intent to turn and tell him to leave.

I turn back to leave and he is there in the doorway his body seeming to fill the entire frame. "I did not follow you here to be insulted." He takes a few steps into the kitchen and I inadvertently take a few steps back as well. He sets his mug on the counter and steps closer effectively cornering and trapping me. "It may be difficult for you to believe, but this is very real. You knew what I was, and had no trouble believing it. Now, I need you to open your mind further and realize that you get no choice in this matter." His hand wraps around my arm once more and I feel heat shoot through me, my breath catching as he leans in closer to press his mouth to my ear.

"This mark means you are mine and you will do as I say."

His mouth moves from my ear to my throat, and his hot breath is almost too much for me to handle. My heartbeat is fast, and my breathing is heavy. In the matter of an instant my body is on fire and wants nothing more than to feel his naked flesh against mine. To fully submit to his power and let him take me in the most primal way.   I try not to move or react to him, but my body has already betrayed me.

His soft chuckle catches me off guard as he releases me and steps back to stare into my eyes again.   "Most people are overcome with fear when I'm that close to them, you really are unique Miss Donovan."   He turns and walks out of the kitchen, leaving me to follow.

"How am I supposed to find your so called son?   I know nothing about you, nor him.   I wouldn't even know where to start looking or who to look for... and why can't you just go find him? You're the demon, I'm just a human."   I walk into the living room to face him but he's gone.   I search the entire apartment and can't find him.   "Son of a bitch," I mutter, shaking my head and putting on my shoes.

Chapter Two

** *Jacki* **

"I don't know Jacki, that sounds pretty crazy, are you sure you weren't just drunk and like, hallucinated or something?" Tera fixed her blonde curls in a security mirror as we walked out of the break room.

"There's no way. I mean, I know the first half was a dream, but what about this fucking tattoo?" I pulled my sleeve up to wave my arm at her, but she quickly dismissed me and kept walking towards the check stands.

"It looks like a fresh tattoo, you probably got it last night after you left the bar. Did you text Robbie? He was bartending last night I'm sure he can fill you in." She gave me one of her signature looks that said the conversation was over before smiling and opening her lane for customers.

I sighed and turned back towards my own check stand, maybe she was right? I rubbed at the spot the tattoo was and tried to put it to the back of my mind.

I'd lived a pretty wild and crazy life at times, but never really had I ever gotten so carried away that something like this had happened. Yeah, I had always heard stories of people getting tattoos while blackout drunk, but I guess I just never thought I would do such a thing. The worst I could recall doing was getting my nose pierced during a couple month coke binge.   A friend at the time had convinced me it would be a good idea, in case some crystals got lodged in the piercing, and later you could get a surprise bump when it finally dislodged. It wasn't my brightest moment, but hey, I never said I was smart in my younger days.

I plastered on my fake retail smile, and kept myself busy the rest of the evening, letting the hours fly by before I found myself back at my employee locker.   I sent out a mass text before pulling my uniform polo over my head.

Me: Party tonight?

I pulled my black misfits shirt from the locker before shoving the work shirt inside.   I always got questionable looks from management when they saw me wad it up into the locker, but no one ever said anything to me.   I guess they didn't wrinkle as bad as normal clothes.

My phone beeped with a few texts, so I slammed the locker closed and hurried down the stairs.

Tera had gotten off a couple hours before me, and of course she was one of the first to respond.

Tera: Riot Room has $1 Shots!! Yessss!!!

I rolled my eyes and moved on to the next message, not bothering to reply to her yet. She knew I'd be there no matter what.

Rob: bands here- $1 shots, should be busy
Me: heading to you then. –how drunk was I last night???

Robbie was one of my best friends and one of the first people I met when I had moved to Kansas City. Granted, his job as a bartender was the reasoning behind meeting him so quickly, but he was the one I grew close to in the couple years I'd been there. He worked at a dive bar that doubled as a local music venue. They didn't always have a show going on but it was our go-to spot when we went out, and Rob put up with our drunken antics.

Rob: U crazy bitch! Tera said u got a tat, WTF?!
Me: I'll be there soon, tell her to shut up!
Dylan: Swimming in pussy!! Groupies galore!

I laughed at the message from Dylan and shoved the phone back in my pocket. It was his typical behavior, but I knew deep down he was really a softie. Deep, deep down, somewhere. At least I hoped I was right, otherwise he was just a sex-obsessed asshat.

I reached my van and debated on going home to change clothes. My phone beeped again as I pulled out of the parking lot, and it took all my self-restraint to pull up to a drive-thru to order dinner before checking the message.

Tera: OMG HOTTIE ALERT! Just showed up-Totes UR type!!! Hurry up BITCH!

I laughed and my decision was made, I would be going home first to lose the work slacks and put on something a little more fun.   I didn't want to completely change clothes, maybe just put on that cute denim short skirt I'd gotten recently. I'd keep my chucks on, and the Misfits shirt, giving me my typical punk-rock, doesn't care what you think, look.

I got my burrito from the window and hauled ass to get home.

Chapter Three

** *Julius* **

I had a stack of test to grade, but they were all at home on my desk, being neglected. Summer term was almost over, just another week until finals, and here I was losing all that valuable time because I promised my friend Dave that I'd come out to his show.

Being the nerd I apparently was, I typically didn't go out much, especially to night clubs or dive bars or whatever this place was supposed to be. Sure, in my younger days, buddies took me out to bars all the time, but that was what people in their early twenties did, wasn't it? College professors pushing thirty had no business out partying all hours of the night.

In fact leaving the house for anything besides work or groceries seemed like a waste of my time. Sure it cut down on my social life but I almost preferred it that way. I always had the lingering feeling that someday I'd have to pack up and leave without a trace, but being almost thirty that hadn't happened yet and I was starting to doubt it ever would.

As if summoned by my thoughts, my phone began playing Witchy Woman by The Eagles. It was my mother calling and I always had to hold in my laughter at my own private joke.   She would be less than pleased if she ever found out what her ringtone was, but I was her son and I got my sense of humor from her.

I fumbled and almost dropped the thing as I pulled it from my pocket.   "Shit," I muttered, the fear of having to deal with another shattered screen was enough to give me nightmares.   I was still a couple blocks from the bar as I slid my thumb across and answered with, "Hey Ma, what's up?"

"Jules! Are you still coming to visit in a couple weeks?"   She sounded excited that I answered as if she hadn't spoken to me in years.   I knew better, we spoke almost every week and I mentally cursed myself for forgetting that she would be calling tonight.

"Of course I am.   What kind of son misses the chance to watch their mother turn 29 again?"   I laughed and jogged across a street, earning a honk from a passing car.

"Don't be an ass Julius Edward!"   Even though she used my middle name I could hear her holding back giggles.   "What are you up to tonight honey?"

I slowed my pace now that I was back on the sidewalk and continued heading south.   "My buddy Dave's band is playing a show tonight so I told him I'd stop by."

"You don't have work to do?"   She sounded suspicious and she knew my work habits. I never went out, ever.

"Of course I have work.   I've got a whole stack of tests to grade and I still need to build the study guides for all my finals next week.   I'll just have to play catch up later.   Dave was, well, he was Dave.   It won't kill me to go out for one night, it's a weekend and I deserve a Friday night off according to him."

I could hear her holding back.   She was the reason I had trust issues and never went out much.

"It very well could kill you, if you ran into the wrong people…" her words came out as a choked whisper, and it took everything I had not to let out the sigh I was holding in.

My mother was a witch.   No, not a bitch, an honest to god witch.   She kept her practicing a secret as long as she could, but I was a curious kid and as much as we moved around growing up her secret didn't stay hidden from me for very long. (She really was going to hate me for my ringtone if she found out.)

When I found out at age nine I was fascinated with her majik but I was also devastated when I didn't have any power of my own.   Years later I found out differently, that she had bound my own majik at birth and spent every waking breath making sure it stayed that way to keep me safe from my father.   He was a man I had never met, never seen a photo of, nor had I ever known his name.

He was supposedly a very powerful, yet dangerous demon.

Any normal boy would have grown up with some sort of complex and maybe had their own mother committed to the looney bin to be locked away for good.   But, not me.

She had proven everything true, time and time again.   I had seen her majik work firsthand and I knew what she was capable of.   I had been exposed to the supernatural world and shown that there were good and bad no matter where you looked.

I chose to avoid it all, and technically I was safer that way.   If my demon father knew of my existence, there was a chance he could be looking for me and the longer I could hide in the human world, the better off I was.

According to my mother, if I fell into the wrong hands, I was a vat of unimaginable power just waiting to be tapped.   Luckily my demon blood was kept dormant, my mother's majik ensured that I appeared entirely human and as long as I didn't try to dabble in majik it would stay that way.

"I know mother," I replied, "after I get grades submitted I'll be down.   Should be about ten days from now."

"I just worry about you Julius," her voice cracked slightly and I hoped she didn't start crying before I was able to hang up.   "You moved two states away and I can't protect you as well when you're gone…"

"I'm fine mother," I tried to sound as reassuring as possible, "your majik is still holding up. There's a werewolf in one of my classes that would have approached me if they thought I wasn't normal." I spotted the club about another block away and my pace sped up.

"I gotta go mom, text me later, okay? I love you."

"Okay… love you too." She sniffled a little but I hit the end call button and shoved the phone back into my jeans.

Yeah, I was a bit of an asshole.

I could hear rock music blaring from the open door as I approached. There was a group of people lined up to get inside while the bouncer was checking IDs and collecting the cover charge. I only waited a couple minutes before I paid my five bucks and was inside, quickly looking to the stage and making sure it wasn't Dave's band.

There was a pretty decent crowd already for only being around nine pm, so it took a few moments to push past the bar line and scan for Dave. After my eyes adjusted I spotted him standing by a table leaned in close to a blonde.

"Jules!" He shouted when I got close, "Son of a bitch! You actually showed!!!" He dropped his beer on the table and grabbed me for a quick hug, his mouth spread into a huge grin.

I laughed and shrugged out of his grasp, "I told you I'd make it man, I'm not a total dick."

Despite his grungy rocker looks, he was one of the best natured and happiest guys I knew. He had long red hair twisted into dreads, a ginger beard to match, and tattoos up and down his arms. He taught guitar at several of the local colleges and gave voice lessons on the side as well. Talent aside, his great personality was likely the reason everyone knew him and got along with him.

The blonde wasted no time, stepping forward and offering her hand to me, "I'm Tera!"

As I greeted her Dave pitched in, "Tera, this here is my good buddy Julius, he teaches at one of the colleges too." He waved his arm in a dramatic flourish and continued, "Jules, this is Tera, my favorite grocery clerk!" He gave her a wink and I watched her try not to blush.

I released her hand and flashed a smile. She was pretty enough, but I could sense a bit of a ditzy air about her. She was more Dave's type than my own, almost high maintenance but she worked hard to not appear to be. Her nails looked freshly done, those long fake things that cost a fortune to upkeep; she had on a lot of makeup and it was enough to make me wonder how much time she spent on her appearance before leaving home each day. Hours, I was betting.

High maintenance women just weren't my thing. Don't get me wrong, I can be shallow as fuck sometimes but a girl confident in her own skin that could throw on a pair of jeans and t-shirt and not worry about her hair or makeup... Well shit, that was sexy as hell.

"What time do you guys go on?" I leaned towards Dave to be heard without yelling. From the corner of my eye, I watched Tera's hands flying over her phone texting someone with a big grin on her face.

"These guys should be done in another half hour then we'll be up, followed by the headliners."

Just then a pitcher of beer and a stack of glasses were dropped onto the table by a man that was a good foot shorter than myself. He had a mix of a goth and punk rock look about him, from the patched up skinny jeans, the black fishnet shirt, the blue mohawk, to his skin covered in tattoos and piercings.

"Teraaaaaa!!!!" he shouted out her name with a smile before picking her up and spinning her around. It made it apparent that he wasn't a scrawny guy. He may have been just barely over five feet tall, but was hiding a lot of muscle beneath the clothes.

She squeaked and playfully slapped him, "Dylan Michael put me down right now!"

He spun her around one more time out of spite before putting her down while laughing the whole time.

She smacked him again on the shoulder for good measure as he turned his attention to David.

"Dave, man! You guy's gotta play here more often, this place is filled with hot ass!"

"We play where we can get in but I don't think I can take credit for all of this crowd, we're not the headliners." He reached forward and took the pitcher from Tera to fill his own glass. "I only hope they invite us back to play again, I always loved this little dive."

"Right on," Mohawk nodded before turning to me and offering his hand. "Hey man, I'm

Dylan."

"Julius," I replied, giving his hand a quick shake.

He offered me a glass as he poured his beer, and I accepted with a nod. Once everyone's glasses were full, he raised his in a toast, "To pussy! I'll be swimming in it tonight!"

"Oh gross!" Tera smacked him on his shoulder as our glasses met, and Dylan proceeded to chug while holding up his middle finger to her.

I took a drink and smiled. It had been a while since I'd had a group of close friends to joke around with like they did. My focus slid towards the band on stage as they announced their last couple songs. They weren't half bad, but as usual they were the opening act so they didn't get as much attention as they deserved.

We all seemed content to listen to the music with our drinks when I noticed Dylan pouring the last of the pitcher into his glass. I reached for the handle and asked, "What was it? I'll get the next one."

"Alright! I knew you seemed legit!" he slapped me on the back before adding, "Its shock top."

I nodded and gave a smile before turning towards the bar. About halfway over my eyes locked with those of a tall brunette. She was leaned over the bar laughing with the bartender and I stopped a moment to just look at her. She was curvy and judging by the way her short denim skirt hugged her ass, she embraced the curves she had.

Tattoos covered her long legs and I chuckled at seeing her converse sneakers as opposed to the heels most other women wore. My eyes trailed back up to her misfits t-shirt with the neckline cut out so that it hung off her shoulders and her arms were covered by long white shirt sleeves beneath.

I continued my walk to the bar as I silently regarded her. Her short brown hair, cut into a bob, bounced as she laughed at something and hopped from foot to foot. She leaned closer and kissed the bartender on the mouth. He immediately wiped it off with a mock disgusted look and shooed her away.

I caught her eyes again as she bound away, her hands full with four drinks. I was about to offer help, but she must have sensed it and chirped, "I got it big boy, you go refill Dylan's beer!"

I blinked at her words and watched her go join the table I had just been at. I smiled at the luck and turned back towards the bar to hand the pitcher over, muttering "shock top" as he took it from me.

The bartender smiled and winked before turning to go fill it. He was a sharp dressed and clean cut black man and based on his interaction with the girl a moment earlier, I was betting he was gay. I paid for the pitcher and made my way back towards the table, noticing that the girl was like a glowing beacon under the black lights.

"My hero!" Dylan shouted as I got close, holding up his empty glass. He filled his own glass as well as mine and Dave's and I noticed the girls each had two drinks and were leaned close talking together.

I could have sworn that Tera pointed at me, but I ignored it and pretended to pay attention to the opening band's last song. I spared a glance at the other girl and noticed she had a lip and septum ring, nothing too brazen like Dylan, he probably had over a dozen piercings just in his face.

The band finished and left the stage and a crew popped in and started tearing down equipment as quick as they could. "Well, I gotta go set up," Dave raised his glass in salute and vanished into the crowd.

Dylan walked away not long after and I assumed he was looking for women. I finished my beer and walked a little closer to the stage to watch as Dave and his bandmates appeared to the sound of cheers and began tuning.

They played their first song and as the last notes ended a beer was pushed into my hand. I looked over and saw the girl smiling at me, with her own beer raised in salute. She winked and turned back towards the stage, cheering and swaying to the music beside me.

I caught myself staring at her and every time she turned my way, I had to act as If I was watching the show. After a few songs, she put her hand on my arm and leaned in to shout in my ear. "It's dollar shots night, come with me!"

I didn't need any more to drink, but her hand on my arm seemed to sizzle through me and I was no longer thinking with my head. I wanted this woman and I hadn't even spoken to her yet.

She led me back to the bar and pushed her ass up against my dick as she leaned over the bar. I took a step back to put the space back between us as she shouted, "Robbie!! We need shots!"

"Wait your turn ya dirty bitch!" He laughed from the other end of the bar and finished waiting on his customers down there.

She laughed as well and then turned towards me. "So," she began, her eyes looking me over from top to bottom, "I'd ask if you came here often, but I know you don't. I'm guessing you're a friend of Dave."

She crossed her arms across her chest before continuing, "He seems like a decent guy, although Tera hardly cares for the good ones, so I've got him pegged as a douchebag rocker. You though, hmmm…" She tapped her finger on her mouth as if she was thinking about what to say next.

"You seem uncomfortable, like you'd rather be anywhere else in the world than in this bar. Yet at the same time, you seem confident and relaxed. You almost have that brooding type vibe, like you have some crazy dark secret…Are you…Batman?!" Her eyes shone as she laughed, and I had to remind myself that she was most likely just a people reader.

"Bitch!" The bartender was back at our end and filling several shot glasses and smiling at us.

"Oh Robbie, you know me so well!" She placed her hands on her heart like it may burst.

It looked like he was pouring vodka, so when he looked at me and asked if I was having the same, I nodded.   I didn't realize what I'd gotten myself into until there were eight shots lined up before us.

I took a deep breath and picked up the first glass, looking at her.   "And if I AM batman?" My words held traces of laughter as I awaited her to raise her glass in response.

"Well, then Gotham is burning tonight, because you are now mine!"   She winked at me and we both slammed all four shots.

By the time Dave's band was finished playing I was pretty buzzed, if not completely drunk. I tried not to let it show, but I was lost dancing with a nameless girl.

I had tried asking her name, but she kept evading me with answers like, "Poison Ivy" or "Cat woman" So I ended up calling her Harley Quinn and she seemed to approve.

The headlining band was playing and the more she danced against me the more my resolve faded.   "I'm going to fuck you tonight," I growled into her ear as her ass rubbed against me again. She stopped where she was and looked up at me, her face overcome with desire.

I grabbed her hand and pulled her outside, opting for a cab instead of walking the mile.   She used the time in cab to straddle my lap as I claimed her mouth with my own.   The car had barely stopped in front of my house before I threw cash at the driver and pulled her out and up the steps.

The door barely closed behind us before I pinned her to the wall and slipped a hand under her skirt feeling her moisture.   Her legs wrapped around me as I picked her up and carried her to the bedroom.

I pushed both of her shirts up over her head, but kept the sleeves in place to use as a quick tie to bind her arms up above her.   I smiled at her lack of a bra and bent down to suck one tight nipple into my mouth.   I gently bit down, pulling away as she gasped from the sensation.   My left hand tweaked the other nipple as my right hand trailed down between her legs again.   Her skirt was bunched up around her hips making it easy to just move her panties aside and dip a finger inside.

She was so wet and hot, crying out at my intrusion.   I looked up and met her eyes as I slid a second finger inside and grazed her clit with my thumb.   Her back arched and she looked down at me as my fingers teased her g-spot and my thumb drew circles on her clit.

I felt her tightening around my hand as her whimpers turned to moans.   "That's right baby, come for me, just like this."   I was sobering up quickly from watching her eyes roll back as pleasure overtook her, and feeling her gush around my hand almost pushed me over the edge as well.

I drew my hand up and tasted her juices as they dripped down my fingers.   "Mmm, you taste pretty fucking good."   I shoved the sticky soaked fingers into her mouth and groaned as she licked them clean.

"Flip over onto your knees," I instructed as I stripped off my own pants and reached into my nightstand to grab a condom. She started to pull the shirts off and I stopped her. "No. Keep those on, I like you restrained."

She obeyed and was on all fours looking back at me over her shoulder. I kneeled behind her and gave her ass a hard slap before yanking off her panties and throwing them across the room. She moaned and I quickly rolled the condom on just before shoving inside her.

She was tight as I slowly withdrew before I teased her by easing back in just as slow.

"Harder!" She begged with a whimper, so I leaned forward and grabbed her wrists where the shirts were tangled around like rope. I hoisted her up and started pounding into her, fucking her like a rag doll, reaching my other hand up to wrap around her throat.

I felt her tighten around my cock as my hold on her throat tightened. "Ooh, you like that, you fucking slut?" I growled into her ear and she nodded, unable to speak.

I released her throat to hold her steady as I continued to pound into her before I shoved her back down onto all fours, getting close to my release. I slapped her ass a few more times leaving bright red handprints, before grabbing her hips and holding her steady as I slammed into her again and again.

Her moans had turned to screams and I felt her orgasm around my cock causing my resolve to break. I groaned as I came, pumping a few more times before riding it out.

I rolled off her to go throw away the condom and came back to find her fast asleep in the center of the bed. She was still fully clothed besides the panties I'd ripped off. I smiled and quickly unlaced her shoes, tossing them to the floor before unzipping her skirt and pulling it off as well. I tried pulling the shirts off her arms but she whimpered, so I popped them back around her head and adjusted them back into place. I yanked my shirt over my head and pulled my boxers back on before climbing into the bed. She sighed as I wrapped my arms around her, pulling her in close before drifting off to sleep beside her. .

I woke up to the sun streaming in through the window and I was completely alone, the rumpled sheets and smell of sex were the only reminder that she'd even been here. I got up and saw a note on the bedside table.

Thanks for the great night Batman!
xxx HQ

I shook my head with a smile and headed for the bathroom, still not knowing her name.

Chapter Four

** *Julius* **

I slammed my laptop shut and walked away from the kitchen table. It had been almost a week since I'd brought the mystery girl home and even though I was typically focused on my work, thoughts of her kept invading my mind. I tried to push her out knowing this was the final week of summer term before I had a couple short weeks off. I had barely managed to get the study guides complete for my students for the final that I was currently trying to finish preparing.

I ran my hands through my hair, knowing full well I needed a haircut soon. Glancing at the clock on the stove I decided to call Dave and see if I could catch him before his nightly visit to the gym.

It rang twice before his voice broke through with a cheery, "Yo?!"

"Hey man, you doing anything tonight?"

"Julius? You okay bro, isn't this a school night?" His laughter eased my nerves a bit, and a smile crept across my face.

"Yes, it's me. I'm just frying my brain trying to get these finals made. I need to let off some steam or something."

"I get it man, that's why I don't teach any

real classes. Fuck, it was rough enough as a student." I could hear his TV in the background, "You wanna hit the gym or go for drinks? There might be a show tonight at riot again."

I held in a sigh, "I don't think drinks will help, I'm behind because of the drinking last Friday."

"Ohhhhh!!!!" He held out the word with a knowing tone, "You're hung up on that chick, aren't ya!?"

I didn't want to admit to it, but he knew me well enough.

"She's a drifter Jules. She never stays anywhere very long. Tera told me that she just rolled into town a few months ago and is still a complete mystery. Never really talks about herself, but she's tagged in a ton of pics on Facebook from parties all across the county." He paused and I heard his TV shut off. "She sounds like bad news man."

"I figured as much but I still need to get out for a while," I had my own secrets, and the last thing I needed was someone sticking their nose into my business asking questions. In all honesty, this girl sounded like exactly what I needed, someone who wouldn't ask questions or expect any sort of long term commitment. "I'm guessing you know her name then, if you've seen her Facebook? She never did tell me…"

My words trailed off as Dave broke off into uncontrollable laughter. It sounded like he was crying from laughing so hard and I contemplated hanging up before he finally regained control and answered me. "You spent all night with the chick and never got her name?" He started laughing again, "Oh shit man, that's great. I'll see you at the gym in twenty minutes!"

He hung up before I could respond, and I was staring angrily at my phone before it chirped with a text.

> *Dave- her name's Jacki Donovan*
> *Dave- be there in 20*

I chuckled and glanced at the computer, debating on pulling up Facebook and looking her up, but then decided against it and grabbed my duffel bag for workouts.

It wasn't like it mattered much anyways, next week I would be heading down to Dallas to visit my mother. Not only was it just a friendly visit, but she used it as an excuse to check her majik over me to be sure I was still passing for human. Call me curious but a part of me wanted the majik to drop just to see what I was capable of, but I also knew there was no going back once that kind of power took hold.

I knew majik only from an observation standpoint by watching my mother practice for many years, but I'd never actually tried it myself.

I would be 30 in a few months and I figured if this so called demon father hadn't come for me yet, that he never would. I was tired of a life of fear and I knew I could never have children without risking them to living with the same fear I was raised with. I just didn't know what else to do.

I was tired of having so many secrets and only having one friend I could really trust. Even then, there were only so many things that we were willing to divulge with one another.

When I had mentioned the werewolf to my mother I hadn't been completely honest. Yes, it was someone at the college, but it wasn't a student or a random faculty member. It was my best friend David.

My thoughts drifted back to the first time I had met him to when I had made my first mistake. I had just moved to Kansas City for this teaching job, purposefully putting some distance between myself and my mother. I didn't expect to run into any supernatural creatures, but I had a few warning charms just in case.

There were a few in-service days a week before fall classes began, and new faculty were encouraged to get to know others during this time. I didn't intend to meet anyone outside of the math department, but somehow I was talked into being introduced to almost everyone in attendance.

The charm inside my wristwatch flared warm to warn me that someone around me wasn't quite human. My heart raced a bit and my breathing hitched as I was introduced to a Mr. David Ward.

"Just Dave," he said with a laugh, his eyes looking me over.

I quickly nodded a hello, "Julius Bennett, please excuse me." I turned to go and made my way back to my office to grab my jacket to leave.

"You don't have to be afraid of me you know," Dave was waiting for me outside my office door.

I was startled and again my heart raced. I took a few calm breaths before he spoke again.

"You panicked when we met, so I'm assuming you have a way of knowing what I am." It wasn't a question, and I debated on whether or not to answer.

"A grungy music teacher?" I tried to joke but I knew I was giving myself away with every beat of my racing heart.

He leaned in close to sniff me as he laughed. "You smell human, no majik…just fear." He was back in his own space and took a step back to try and ease my mind. "You need to get that heart rate under control, it's what gave you away. I can tell how fucking terrified you are, chill bro."

I glanced around the hallway seeing a few others heading towards this row of offices, "I don't know you and I'm not sharing any secrets here. This is hardly the place for this kind of discussion."

He looked towards the approaching group and laughed before extending his hand. "I'm Dave Ward, guitar teacher, vocal coach, musician, and a big ginger puppy!"

I only hesitated half a second before taking his hand. "Julius Bennett, math teacher, son of a witch."

The last part took him by surprise and he was howling with laughter as the group passed us by. "Do you drink?" he asked as his laughter turned to a smile. "There's a bunch of bars not too far off, we could grab a few rounds and decide whether to talk or not."

I'm not sure where my sudden trust came from but I went and we became good friends. Although he was a werewolf, he was a good man that ran with a small pack of a few other good guys. He shared enough about himself so that I felt safe and I told him about my paranoid mother that warded me at birth to try and live a "normal" life.

Neither of us gave away all of our secrets, but it was a mutual trust we shared and I knew that if my majik ever wore off he would tell me. It wasn't much of a surprise when three years later he was still my closest friend in Kansas City.

I arrived at the gym about the same time that he did. I grabbed my bag and followed him inside, stopping at the locker room to change. We met on the indoor track on the second floor and did a few stretches before setting into an easy jog.

We didn't need to talk, we'd have time for that later if needed. He slowly picked up the pace, pushing me to go faster until he knew I was at my fastest. A few laps continued like that before he glanced back at me and then took off in a blur.

"Oh, come on! That's cheating!" I shouted, slowing back down to a jog.

He appeared next to me and matched my

pace while laughing. I shook my head as I finished into a walk before I grabbed my towel to wipe the sweat from my face. I tossed it to Dave like usual and reached for the door to head down to the weight room.

Before I could push it open, Dave was there pulling it closed and blocking my way.

"Jules," he was holding the towel and looking at me in a very serious manner. "Have you been around demons lately?"

I'd been practicing at remaining calm since our meeting three years prior, but I knew that I was lucky to have the run as an excuse for my heart to already be racing. My stomach dropped a bit as I kept my cool, "Not that I know of, why?"

He was never a serious person but the look he was giving me right that moment was terrifying. "You smell different Jules... you smell like demon."

He stared at me a moment longer before shoving the towel into my hand and darting out the door.

"Fuck," I muttered, my panic rising as I took off after him.

He hadn't left, but he was clearly pissed off on one of the weight benches. I sat down at the leg press near him as he continued his reps.

"I thought you were just a half breed witch, why do you smell like demon?" His voice was just above a whisper to keep others from hearing us.

The gym was pretty empty at this hour but there were still a few people scattered around, most of them with headphones on working out to their own rhythm.

"I'm not a demon," my answer was pointless but I wasn't sure how to reply. I glanced around again before continuing. "My mother is a witch, I've always been honest about that, but I've never known my father. All I know is that he is…was… a powerful demon. My entire life has been spent moving around, being subjected to mom's paranoid majik binding. She was always worried that he would try to come find me."

Dave stopped his reps and sat up to stare at me as I continued. "As far as I know, this is the first time I haven't passed for 100% human… I need you to tell me how strong the scent is, how obvious it is. I'm going to Texas next week, but if I need to go sooner, I need to know now."

"Didn't you just go down right before summer term?" He was right and he knew that I tried to visit my mother a couple times a year. There was no reason the majik should be weakened.

"It isn't that strong of a scent," he continued as he got up to switch machines. "If it hadn't been for that towel, I don't think I would have noticed. I can't smell it from where I am now, if that helps."

We both remained silent the rest of our workouts as we put our aggression into the weights. It wasn't until we had cleaned up that Dave spoke again as we approached our separate vehicles.

"There hasn't been any demon activity around here recently, and now that you're showered

I really can't smell anything." His grin was back as he said, "as long as you avoid getting all hot and sweaty, you should be okay for another week."

I breathed a sigh of relief and thanked him before his signature grin spread even wider.

"So... You going to look up that girl?"

I smiled, Dave's good nature bringing my own humor back out, "She's the least of my worries right now. She can keep her secret drifter life, I've apparently got daddy issues."

My mother would be hysterical when I showed up with her majik worn off, especially since it had only been two months since my last visit. Something was wrong and I only hoped it wasn't anything too terrible.

Chapter Five

*** Jacki ***

My head throbbed from a hangover as I drove to campus. It had been almost a month since the tattoo showed up on my arm and every night after I partied hard, throwing myself into the liquor with more strangers than friends. It was starting to seem more like a distant dream and I was happy with that.

Tera had bugged me a few times about the guy I hooked up with, telling me his name was Julius and that she could ask Dave for his number if I wanted it. I wound up quitting my job just to have an excuse to avoid her constant prodding.

I'll admit, the sex was hot and something about him lit a fire inside of me. More times than I could count, I'd wake up in the morning flushed from hot and filthy dreams about him.

I was someone that didn't date, I didn't get involved. Becoming attached to someone was just asking for trouble and emotions were ugly. I was still a nomad at heart, and even though I'd started planting roots here in Kansas City the idea of leaving danced in the back of my mind.

Working a job wasn't that difficult, it paid the bills and gave me an excuse to stay a little while, but signing up for college classes was the most terrifying thing I had done in a while.

I think I was trying to prove to myself that I could do it, that I could settle down and live like a normal person. But I missed the traveling, life on the road seeing new places all the time… nothing was ever enough.

I didn't have any family to speak of, growing up I had only had a mother when she felt like being around, which wasn't very often. It was a few months before my 18th birthday that I came home from school and found her unconscious on the kitchen floor.

She was an alcoholic so I was used to the sight, but this time there was a note.

Every day you
look more like HIM
I can't take it anymore
you're gonna be just like him
blood sucking demon

The writing had been choppy and hard to read, but I remembered the words clearly. I was angry at her and she was still barely alive when I found her.

I screamed.

I cried.

But I didn't phone the police… I wanted her to just die.

I collapsed in the corner, crying hot angry tears while waiting and watching her until she started vomiting and choking on her own bile. I watched her die and I felt nothing.

I sat there in a daze for hours until night came. I was certain what happened next was real, but anyone I had ever told dismissed it as a shock induced hallucination. I looked at the police report a few months later and it clearly said that I had been the one to call emergency services, there was even a transcript of the call but I didn't remember any of it.

I saw my father that night, for the first and only time in my life. He showed up while I was still huddled in the corner and stood in the doorway looking at my mother's corpse. My tears had long since stopped and I was simply holding my legs to my body while staring at her lifeless body. He must have been there for several minutes before I looked up and saw him.

He could have been my older brother, he looked so young. "She said I looked like you…" I whispered not able to find any other words.

"I am so sorry, my sweet child." His voice was calm and soothing as he knelt down beside me. He placed a hand on my back and the other under my legs, scooping me up and carrying me to bed. "Go to sleep and dream of happier times."

I drifted off to sleep but there were no happy memories awaiting me, only the haunting visions of my mother.

Several days after her death a lawyer called informing me of accounts in my name that I needed to come sign for. My mother had no estate to speak of; I had been working under the table to support myself since I was fourteen, and then had two full time jobs as well as school after I was sixteen. I had been paying the bills and keeping a roof over my own head for years before she had finally killed herself.

I knew the money was a ruse, some sort of payoff from my absent father. My mother wouldn't have been around at all if she had access to millions of dollars in a bank account. So I knew, deep down, it was from him as a way of apologizing for not being around my life.

I didn't touch the money at first, almost sickened by the idea of being paid off. I kept working both jobs until I finished high school and graduated. After my hours were cut at one job, I snapped and quit both of them.

I stopped paying rent, breaking the lease and bought a van instead. Almost everything I owned was able to fit in it, so I packed up what I could and started driving west until the road ended at the ocean.

I spent three days just sitting in the sand watching the waves come in before I started meeting the street kids. They weren't all kids technically but they lived on the streets and it was a magical experience to me. They weren't enslaved to the typical way of life everyone else was.

I probably spent a year at Venice Beach drinking wine from space bags, going to parties near the canals or singing at celebrities that walked past us on the boardwalk. I was finally free and living a life I enjoyed.

I saw all Hollywood had to offer and then began traveling all along the west coast, my van loaded with new friends.   I still hadn't touched the blood money, but my own savings were running low after buying the van and heading west.   The street kid life worked and I quickly learned how to gas jug to keep traveling or how to fly a sign for spare dollars or change.

Years passed that way, sleeping in national parks, beaches, in the van, or even splurging for a hotel on special occasions.   Every so often a group would have a house or apartment but I'd never stay any place for very long, six months at most.

After about five years of it, I settled down a bit more.   I'd find a room to rent, get a job, and stay eight or nine months.   Las Vegas, New York, Miami, Portland, Dallas, and then I wound up in Kansas City.

I had dipped into the account a few times, usually to splurge on big parties.   I'd never let anyone know where the money had come from, not wanting to abuse the privilege, but deep down I knew I was living a lie.

I wasn't the only one, I knew for a fact that a few other street kids came from money but chose to turn from it.   When it came down to it, all they had to do was go home to mommy or daddy and then they would be able to afford to hits the streets again in no time.

It was hard to stay in one place now that I had traveled all around, but I was trying.   I went back to Venice before coming to KC and it just didn't feel the same.   So many things had changed and we had all gotten older.   The beach was different, the boardwalk was crawling with police and our hill was gone.   I stayed a couple weeks trying to see any familiar faces before leaving for good to plant myself somewhere new.

So essentially I could say that I had my street family, but I'd never really have a place to call home.

The night the demon had appeared in my dream and my home had reminded me of my mother's death all over again.   I knew he wasn't the same man as my father but the memories still resurfaced and it didn't surprise me that I threw myself back into the downward spiral of endless parties.

I had only had the one hookup with the sexy and aggressive Julius, but no others really seemed interesting enough.   So when Tera kept pushing the topic of seeing him again I instead decided to quit my job and drink myself numb.

I pushed the thoughts of my mother out of my head and found a parking space on the roof of the parking garage.   My messenger bag was slung over my shoulder and I pushed my sunglasses up closer to my face as I made my way across campus to my first class since high school almost ten years ago.

Algebra.   I had no idea why I signed up for it.   I could have taken something easy, but instead

I chose math and tested out higher than I anticipated.

I was hoping there wouldn't be a lecture since it was the first day, especially with the hangover I was nursing, but I rarely had such good luck.

At least I was still early enough that only one other person was in the classroom. I took a seat in the back corner while putting my earbuds in, and leaned back listening to some Frank Ocean while waiting for class to begin. I took a swig from my water bottle and let the sweet wine coat my throat.

I knew I needed to cut back on the drinking, especially with school starting but it had been a rough few days of nightmares and it was a quick hangover cure.

My head was leaned against the wall as the room slowly filled with students. I was able to study them all from behind my shades and I noticed the class was filled with mostly young girls who seemed to be focused on sitting as close to the front as possible.

I took my earbuds out to try and listen to their conversations, but only had a few moments before the instructor walked in with his arms overloaded with papers and a coffee balanced in his hand.

"Hey guys, sorry I'm late! There was a line at the copy machine and I figured you'd want the lecture outline for today."

"Shit." I must have said it aloud because

half the class turned and looked at me. The instructor was the man I had hooked up with and been fantasizing about, Julius.

He set down his coffee and papers while looking around the room. His gaze lingered over me for only a brief second before he looked back down and held up one stack of papers. "If someone wants to pass these out, I'll take roll and then we can get started."

One of the young girls in the front jumped up immediately, "I'll do it Mr. Bennett!" She acted overly flirty and I had to keep myself from laughing at the scene.

I leaned back again and was glad I still had my shades on. His name was Julius Bennett, and judging by all the girls in the front two rows he had a reputation as the hot teacher.

He started calling out names, making eye contact with each student before moving on. "Jacqueline Donovan?" He looked directly at me waiting for my reply.

"It's Jacki."

A smirk crossed his face as he stared at me and then wrote something down, "I'll take note of that Miss Donovan." His tone was teasing and blondie handing out the papers stood before me at that exact moment. She dropped one in front of me just far enough out of reach that it sailed to the floor.

"Oops," she said smiling, acting like it had been a mistake as she turned back around and went to her seat. If only she knew that I'd already had what she wanted.

This was going to be a long semester if these jealous girls all stuck around.

"Alright guys, I know this is the first day, but we have got a lot to cover. We're going to be here the whole two hours, so if you have your books you should get them out. We'll take a short break in about an hour, but let's go through the syllabus first.

"The first page is the basic stuff, when the class meets, my office number and hours. The second page has the schedule for this whole semester broken down by week and chapter. Highlight the due dates if you need to…"

I followed along for a while as he went on about the grading scale and the school regulations. It was basic mind numbing stuff and I highlighted the important bits like the exam dates.

I may have been a mess the past few weeks, but I was someone that secretly craved structure and stability. I loved to learn, whether reading books, watching documentaries, or solving math equations, I was a bit of a nerd in that aspect. I knew I would find a routine soon to focus my energy on school work.

When Julius started the lecture on chapter one the majority of the class groaned, whilst I was already looking ahead to see what I remembered and began taking my own notes.

Another stack of handouts went around that included the homework assignments for every section we would cover in class. I focused my attention towards the board as he did a few examples and worked through them painstakingly slow with detailed explanations of each step.

His voice became almost soothing background noise as I started in on the homework, not realizing everyone had gone to break until the door slammed shut and I was alone in the room.

Well, almost alone.

"You didn't combust into flame by telling me your name, so I'd say it wasn't a bad thing to share." Julius was standing at the end of my aisle and I was able to fully look him up and down. His grey shirt sleeves were unbuttoned and rolled up to his elbows, his muscled forearms bare and bulging as they crossed in front of his chest.

My gaze started to travel down towards his snug fit blue jeans, but I stopped myself and rose to my feet, intending to leave the room without a word.

A smile crept across his face as he watched me approach, and I wondered if he was going to let me pass by. I got a step away from him before his stance shifted just enough to block my way.

His arms dropped from his chest and one went to the wall beside me essentially caging me in. His body language showed annoyance as his smile vanished and his words came clipped and harsh. "Do you intend to always come to school hungover, Miss Donovan?"

I lifted the sunglasses from my face and met his gaze only inches from mine. "Do you always have a posse of teenage girls Professor Bennett?"

I tried to add a trace of humor to my tone but my words were just a tad too clipped.

"Jealous?" he asked, stepping closer and forcing me back a few steps until my back was to the corner again.

I remained silent as my body started to react to him being so close. His tongue darted out to lick his lips and suddenly the tension was very clear between us.

"Over half of them will drop this class by next week, the curriculum is not easy and I don't teach gossip 101." His eyes darted down to the table and a satisfied smirk formed as he leaned away from me to take a closer look at the work I'd been doing.

I quickly slammed the book shut, "I guess I should have paid more attention to what classes I signed up for. I could have saved myself some trouble." My tone was bitchy, and the smirk fell as his expression darkened.

"There's still time to switch classes," he leaned back in close and spoke low directly into my ear. "I hear it's frowned upon to fuck my current students and I can guarantee that I will have you again soon Jacki."

I gasped, not meaning to, but it was reflex. My body was already reacting to him and I had to swallow several times before I could form a reply. "I could turn you in for sexual harassment." The words came out barely a whisper.

"You could," he whispered back, "but I could also have you expelled for alcohol on school grounds." He picked up my water bottle to prove his point and opened the lid to give it a whiff.

"You're a fucking dick!" I pushed him away and dropped my sunglasses back onto my face.

"Yeah, but you seemed to enjoy it last time." He opened my textbook and pointed to the problem I had been working on. "This formula is wrong." He turned and walked out of the room without another word and I was left staring angrily down at my textbook as students began filing back in.

I fixed the mistake and soon he was back in the room continuing the lecture without a second glance in my direction. About ten minutes before class was due to end I packed my things up so I would be ready to leave the moment he finished.

I got to my van and shot Tera an angry text.

Me- why didn't u tell me he was a math teacher at my school?!?!!

She wasn't at work today so her reply was almost immediate.

Tera- WHO?

Me- Julius.

Me- he's my algebra teacher…

Tera- HAHA! Oh SHIT!!! Can I still sign up?!

Me- very funny! This is sooo fucked

I slumped forward and banged my head on the steering wheel. "Uuugh," I groaned. "What am I gonna do?"

Chapter Six

*** Jacki ***

I thought about dropping the class or switching to a different professor, but it seemed like a cop out. I'd made the decision to stay in town and get my life on track by going to school, and something like this wasn't going to be enough to derail that plan.

So what if I had slept with the guy? I had chosen to remain anonymous, and obviously that had been a mistake, because now I was in his class unknowingly. I either had to pretend I had no interest in him at all, or play his little game and see him again.

I was a bit of a coward though, so I took the easy route of avoidance. I arrived to class a little late, left a little early, and stayed out of the room during breaks. A few times he tried to catch my gaze, but he knew what I was up to, and he let me play it my way for a while.

Six weeks into the semester he caught me in the hallway in a completely opposite wing of the building. I had my earbuds in and a book to my nose, the world was completely tuned out. I was in the music building and thought I'd be able to have some peace, until one of the earbuds was plucked from my ear and I jumped in surprise.

Julius was sitting beside me on the bench, and his hand came down and gave my thigh a gentle squeeze so I wouldn't dart off.

"What the fuck dude?!"   I hit pause on my music and slid the bookmark in to save my place.

He chuckled, "Good afternoon Miss Donovan.   Do you have any plans this evening?"

"I don't date."   My words were quick and his eyes sparkled with amusement as he watched me.

"I didn't ask you on a date."

"Yes, I have plans."   It wasn't a complete lie, Tera had invited me out to see a show but I'd blown off giving her an answer.

"That almost sounds like a lie and I would appreciate honesty."   He leaned in closer against my side and his breath was warm on my neck as he spoke into my ear, "I don't *date* either, but I think you and I can come to an arrangement.   I won't ask any questions about you and you won't ask any of me.   No commitment.   No promises.   No questions."

"Why would I agree to that?"   I made sure to keep looking straight ahead, not risking turning towards him with his lips already so close to my skin.

"You're a drifter Jacki.   You never get attached because someday you'll get bored and leave.   You may be trying to stay here now but you crave the excitement and the thrill of the open road. I don't expect you to stay."

His words rang true as I turned to face him and I wondered how he knew so much about me. He may be willing to have this arrangement now, but down the line how would he really feel when I left? What if I was the one who got attached?

My eyes searched his, our faces only an inch apart, yet before I could ask him how he knew me so well someone hollered "Yo Jules!"

I pulled away and turned to see the ginger musician Tera had been seeing, David. He held a suit jacket in his hand as he walked towards us, and I almost giggled at the thought of this grungy rocker ever wearing something so nice.

"Bro, you gotta stop leaving your clothes in my classroom." He tossed the jacket at Julius and turned to me, "Hey Jax, you coming to the show tonight? I'm pretty sure I've talked Jules here into making an appearance, but he'll use any excuse to stay home and grade papers or some shit..." Suddenly the gears in my head that had been turning clicked into place.

"You!" I accused, pointing at Dave. "Tera must have opened her big mouth to you, and then you told this guy!"

Dave held his hands up in surrender, "Calm down firecracker! The only thing I've ever told him about you, was your name! Shit dude, I'm not one to run my mouth about anyone else's business."

I almost felt bad for half a second for accusing him, he really did seem like a genuinely nice and honest guy. "I gotta get across town to my other class, I'll see you both tonight?" He looked at me and I couldn't help but say yes.

"Yeah, Tera's been bugging me about it for a week, I'll be there." I grabbed my messenger bag from the bench and slung it over my shoulder as I looked to see what Julius would answer.

He slipped his jacket on while speaking, "I'll come, just don't expect me to stay all night."

Dave grinned, "No problem man! See you guys tonight then!" He turned and went back down the hall leaving me alone with Julius again.

I started to walk the opposite direction, and Jules kept pace by my side. "We all have our secrets Jacki, your adventures just happen to be posted all over Facebook." He stopped me before I got to the nearest door, sensing I was going to try and flee.

His left arm wrapped around my waist as his right hand held the back of my head and he pulled my lips to his. It was a fierce kiss, full of heat and unspoken promises as his tongue darted in and teased my own.

He pulled away just as quickly as he had claimed me and met my eyes while I was still dazed. "Think about it?" and with a wink he spun around and walked down the corridor.

Sonuvabitch, I thought to myself.

His kiss did exactly what he had planned for it to do and he plagued my thoughts the rest of the afternoon. When Tera showed up at my apartment to pick me up for the show I still wasn't dressed or ready to go.

Did I want to see him tonight? Or better

yet, did I want to see him naked tonight? Was I going to go home with him?

I had been spinning through the same thoughts for hours and still hadn't made any solid progress. I knew one thing for sure though, if this were to happen, whatever it was, it would be on my terms and it would be sober. I wouldn't allow him to make the rules, if I went to see him I'd leave when I wanted. I didn't want there to be any time for anything more than a physical arrangement.

I could hear Tera rummaging through my kitchen and I knew she was helping herself to my liquor. She gave a low whistle when I walked in finally dressed.

"You planning on getting it in tonight Jacki?" she teased.

I laughed and sent her a wink, knowing I had made up my mind with the same short denim skirt I had worn the first time I had met Julius. The weather was getting cooler, so I had a few layers on as far as shirts go, but my long legs were bare from the skirt to my Chuck Taylor shoes. I had no intention of going home with him, but a quick bathroom hookup? That was a maybe.

I put my hand on my hip as Tera poured a few more shots into her glass. "We going or not bitch?!"

She took a swig and then skipped down the hall to my bathroom. "Just gotta check my hair and face!"

I went to put the booze away and took a sip from her cup. Holy crap it was strong. I smiled to myself as I picked it up as well as her purse and stood by the door. "Come on bitch, I've got your shit!"

She came back up the hall in a flash of giggles and snagged the cup from my hands. I tried to let her good mood rub off on me, knowing it was best if I stayed positive all night.

The music was loud at this bar, even when the bands weren't playing there was a DJ spinning tunes to pass the time. I had one beer when I arrived but nothing else the rest of the night; I wanted a clear head if Julius showed up.

Dave's band was good and I soon found myself lost in the music. A pair of hands landed on my hips from behind and I instinctively pulled them away before turning to see who it was.

Julius, in plain blue jeans and a fitted black t-shirt. *Jesus, this man looks good no matter what he's wearing.* I gazed at him for a few moments before turning back to the stage.

He stood at my back, yet kept his hands off me. I should have been happy that he was respecting my wishes, but at the same time it was driving me crazy. I wanted his hands on me, and I couldn't focus on the music any longer.

I took a half step back, pressing my body into his until he took the hint and his hands went back to my hips. His head dipped down so he could press his lips to my throat and I lost all my control.

All day he had tormented me with that kiss, and now I had to do something about it. I grabbed his hand and pulled him towards the bathrooms. One of the doors opened right as we approached and I gave a smile to the guy walking out as I dragged us both in and locked the door behind me.

"Jacki…"

"Shut up." I reached for the button of his jeans, "You said no question, and no commitments, so we're going to play this my way. Keep your mouth shut and let me do what I need to do right now, because you're driving me fucking crazy."

I met his gaze for a few moments and his silence gave me the answer I needed. He would let me play it my way for now, giving me the illusion of control, but I still remembered the first night with him clearly in my mind; I knew how aggressive and dominant he really was.

Chapter Seven

** *Jacki* **

A month went by and we continued to play my way, meeting somewhere for drinks or at one of Dave's many shows. We would both sneak off to the bathroom, a supply closet, parking lot, a back alley, anything that was convenient at the time. It was almost as if we were having an affair, but I could tell he was starting to want more.

So when I received a text during thanksgiving break with only his address and a time, I knew the game was changing and it scared me.

I was nervous as I parked in his driveway. I took a few moments to just breathe before finally getting out and walking up to his door. I yanked my coat tighter around myself as I looked up to the sky. It hadn't started snowing yet, but the weather predicted a storm coming soon.

I knocked on the door and waited, the brisk air blowing my hair into my face. A minute passed before I knocked again.

No answer. *What the hell?* I checked my phone and saw that I was fifteen minutes early. *Shit.* I pounded my fist on the door before deciding to just try the knob.

It was unlocked, so I opened it enough to poke my head in as the wind pushed at me again. "HELLO??" I hollered in and then realized there was music playing just loud enough to probably muffle my voice.

"It's fucking cold out here Julius, I'm coming in!" There wasn't an answer so I went in and shut the door firmly behind me.

The house smelled like he had been cooking, and I made my way up the hallway, checking the kitchen before heading towards the bedrooms.

I stood in his doorway and listened to the shower running. No wonder he didn't answer the door. I leaned against the door frame and shouted his name.

There was a loud thud as something crashed to the floor, followed by a "Fuck!"

"Jacki?"

"I would hope so, unless you always leave your door unlocked for various women to come over."

He laughed and I was oh so very tempted to go into the bathroom to see him. "You're early, I'll be right out!"

I stayed there in the doorway as the water finally shut off and the curtain was pulled aside. I could barely see his outline in the fogged up mirror. He appeared in the doorway as he dried himself with a blue towel and I knew I was in for trouble when he smiled at me. My heart sped up and suddenly I was all nerves, it was too intimate watching him and red flags went up as I felt the emotion creep in.

He wrapped the towel around his waist and walked towards me. My feet were planted to the ground and I couldn't move as he reached me and unzipped my coat, tossing it to the side. As if magnetized his hands immediately grasped my hips and pulled me close as he kissed me slow and sensual.

The kiss deepened as his hands slid to my ass, lifting me up as my legs wrapped around him as natural as the many times it had happened the month before. He took a few steps until my back was pressed against the wall, pinning me all while his mouth still expertly invaded my own.

He pulled away from the kiss, both of us breathless as he still held me. One of his hands moved to caress my face, "Fuck Jacki, you are so beautiful."

My heart melted a little more as he kissed me again, slowly lowering me back to my feet. He stepped away and picked up the towel that had fallen away at some point.

"I'm going to put on some clothes. I made some pizza and figured we could watch a movie or something."

"This sounds a lot like a date Julius…" my tone held a warning and my eyes narrowed at him.

"It's not a date. I just thought we could do things a little differently today."

"By cooking me dinner and suggesting we snuggle up and watch a movie?" I leaned down to

63

grab my coat off the floor. "You said no commitment, no questions and no strings. This is too far and I'm not doing it."

"Jax…" His voice was soft as he used my nickname and took a step towards me.

"No Julius. I can't do it. You said it yourself, I'm toxic. I'm going to leave again someday and now you're trying to get attached and change me. Well good job, consider me gone."

I turned to go, hoping to hold in my tears at my own self destructive actions but then he grabbed my arm and everything changed.

His hand wrapped around my forearm right where the strange tattoo resided. The breath was pulled from my body as white hot searing pain erupted from the spot and sent Julius flying back across the room. I could only stand there for a few moments as sparks and colored smoke flew from the tattoo to his crumpled body on the floor.

I willed my body to move to him to check if he was alive. At that moment I knew it was real. All the strange occurrences in my life, the demon visiting me and marking me; I was terrified.

Panic set in as the tattoo continued to grow hotter and I looked around unsure of what to do. "STOP IT!" I screamed at the tattoo, pushing my other hand over it. It immediately went cold and I knew I had to run.

I pulled my coat on and ran back out the front door to jump into my van. My hands started shaking as I tried to put the key in the ignition. I took a deep breath and managed to calm down enough to get it started.

I drove like a mad woman at first, weaving in and out of traffic to get to the highway. I knew it was reckless and the last thing I needed was to accidentally kill myself so I managed to slow down slightly.

I ran the light by the stadiums and pulled into my own driveway after drifting around a few turns. I bolted inside hoping to pack a few essentials before hitting the road, but he was here sitting in my chair just like the first time.

I turned to go back out the door but two men blocked my way. I considered trying to force my way past but their eyes flashed red and the thought left my mind.

"Miss Donovan," the man called from my living room, "please come have a seat."

I pulled my coat tighter around myself and stared up at my ugly water stained ceiling. "What do you want?" I didn't want to face him and I definitely didn't want to sit down. I was mad and I wanted answers.

"You are a very interesting person Miss Donovan and I'm glad to see that you've been quite busy since we last met. I had hoped you hadn't forgot about our little agreement." He almost sounded amused and I found myself stepping back into the same room.

"What agreement?" I ripped my coat off and threw it onto the floor as I held out my tattooed arm. "You put a fucking tattoo on my arm and told me to find some guy with no info or details, and when I tried to ask anything more you vanished like a fucking fart in the wind!"

Okay, so maybe I needed to calm down before making any more Shawshank references, but I hated that I was in this mess. "That's not an agreement, that's a fucking nightmare."

He chuckled as he uncrossed his legs and leaned forward. "You still found him. That tattoo on your arm is my mark and reacts to my blood, all he had to do was touch it and all his precious warding was gone."

"Why would it react to his touch now and not several times before?" My mind was spinning trying to figure it out. Julius had touched me numerous times before today, yet the tattoo had never done this.

"He's never touched the mark before today. He may have lightly brushed it once after I placed it upon you, I felt it very faintly then."

"Yes he has... That doesn't make any sense." My mouth snapped shut as I thought more about it. I had almost always worn long sleeves around Julius; anytime we had been intimate our clothes hadn't come fully off. The more I thought about it, the more I realized the demon was right. Julius had never touched my tattoo before today.

I was silent a while before looking at him and whispering. "Does he know any of this?"

"That's the joy of it! I have no idea how much he knows, but I'll find out soon enough thanks to you."

"No"

"Pardon?"

"No. I didn't agree to this. I'm not just going to hand an innocent man over to someone like you."

"Someone like me?" I didn't see him move from the chair but he was suddenly standing right before me. "Darling, you have no idea who I even am. I'm not just any demon from the Haelexii realm. I'm The King baby, and I always get what I want. Including my son."

I didn't know what to do. Even though I had tried not to get attached to Julius I still had feelings that had started to develop. Feeling I had tried to avoid by leaving him today, before he had grabbed my arm.

"I don't want to do this to him...he doesn't deserve this."

"It's already been done Miss Donovan. You've played your part."

I had to tell him, had to warn him... I turned back towards the door hoping to force my way out to find Julius and apologize.

I didn't make it two steps before the other two demons stopped me. I fought against them trying to get away as they picked me up and carried me back to their king. "LET ME GO! YOU BASTARD THIS IS BULLSHIT!!!"

Each one had a tight grip on one of my arms to keep me from wiggling free as their king stared at me.

"Shut up."

My body did obeyed even though my mind

continued to scream.   My mouth wouldn't open, and I couldn't make any sounds at all.

"You've obviously grown fond of my son and I can't have you running back to him before I'm ready to collect him.   So it looks like I'm going to have to take you with me.   That's not going to be a problem is it?"

I was still unable to speak from whatever spell or command he had put on me.

"Very good."   He placed a hand on my shoulder and my body went limp.   "Boys, make a mess.   I'm going to take this princess back home with me."

NO no no!!!   I couldn't move, I couldn't speak.   I was trapped in my own body and had no way out.   The demons were taking me and I couldn't do anything about it.

How did I get myself into this mess?   I was trying to straighten myself out and live a normal life. I wanted to be ordinary, to be boring... but I couldn't escape it.   My life had always been hell and the past ten years had finally been an escape, a breath of fresh air.

"You're going to sleep now Miss Donovan. I'll need you to be my pawn for a little while longer. Say goodbye to Earth realm, it may be a while before you get to come back."

He scooped me up and my eyes started to drift closed.   I saw the other two demons start trashing my house as everything went black.

Chapter Eight

** *Julius* **

"Wooo-oooh witchy woman... See how high she flies... Wooo-oooh witchy woman... She got the moon in her eyes..."

The ringing in my ears died down enough that I could hear The Eagles singing from the other room. My arms were heavy as I lifted my hands to my head.

The song started again and I groaned. It was my mother calling and I couldn't seem to move to go answer. My eyes opened and everything slowly came into focus.

What had happened? I was naked on my bedroom floor, a towel inches away from my body. I moved my hands up from my face and felt my hair was still wet.

I tried to think back but my head was throbbing. Jacki had been here and I pissed her off; that much I remembered. Did she Taser me?

My phone started ringing again with the same ringtone. She never called this many times in a row.

I groaned again as I crawled to the edge of my bed to help pull myself up.

The song began again and I swayed on my feet as I stood. I took a few shaky steps before I was steady on my feet again. I plopped down on the couch and grabbed my phone from the coffee table. The ringing started again and I finally answered.

"Yeah?" My voice cracked and I could hear sobbing on the other end.

"Julius! Oh my gods! My baby! You're alive!" Her cries were frantic as I tried to formulate a response.

"Of course I'm alive. Why, what's wrong?"

Her sobs got worse and I struggled to understand her.

"Oh my precious baby, I thought I lost you... The majik...I felt it snap...I..." She broke into hysterics again and I couldn't understand a word.

"Mom!" I shouted across the line at her to no avail. "Maria Elena Rose Bennett!"

Using her full name got her attention and the sobs turned to quiet sniffles after a few moments as she tried to calm down.

"You felt my majik snap? When?"

"Just a little bit ago. It felt like you died, it was so quick." She blew her nose before continuing, "What happened to you, what were you doing just before I called?"

"I don't remember really. I had a woman over but I pissed her off and she left. I'm pretty sure she used a Taser on me, I remember reaching for her and then I woke up on the floor to you calling me a million times."

She grew deathly quiet for a moment, "Julius, did she have any tattoos? Any Latin words or strange symbols?"

I ran my free hand through my hair. "I don't know Ma, she had a lot of tattoos, but I don't remember seeing any Latin."

"I'm sending you a picture right now. It's a demonic symbol, I need you to look at it and tell me if you've seen it anywhere at all lately." Her words were hushed and quick. She was afraid and a sinking feeling was developing in my gut.

My phone beeped and I pulled it away from my ear. The image loaded and I took a moment to study it. It looked like three V's expanded outward to form a circular type pattern with their points meeting in the center, with vine like lines twisted around and between the letters.

It looked familiar, but I couldn't place it. I put the phone back to my ear. "I don't know Ma, it almost looks familiar but I don't remember seeing it."

"You need to try and remember Julius. That symbol is the mark of your father; if you were to touch an active mark, no amount of majik could protect you." She paused for only a moment, "Are you sure this girl didn't have the symbol as a tattoo?"

My mind flashed back to when I had grabbed her arm. That symbol had been exactly where my hand had grasped. The memory came flooding back.

I grabbed her arm and the tattoo burned my hand, sparks shot up my arm and flung me back. I had heard a voice whisper through my mind before I blacked out, "I found you."

I let out a shaky breath. "If someone does have this mark, what does that mean?"

"It would mean that they work for the ruler of the Haelexii Realm, and the demon Maxx has his sights set on you finally."

"I've got to go mom. I'll call you tomorrow."

"Jules… I'm not ready to lose you, please tell me she doesn't have the mark."

"I can't tell you either way Mother. Goodnight." I ended the call and turned the device off.

I was betrayed.

White hot rage filled me as I wondered how long Jacki had been working against me. Playing hard to get, trying to stay away… it was all a fucking game to get me closer.

I got up and went to the bedroom to get my clothes on. As I stood at my dresser I caught my reflection in the mirror and my eyes were glowing demon red. I counted to ten, willing myself to calm down as I slowed my breathing. I hoped they would change back and eventually it worked.

I wondered what to do next. I couldn't face Jacki right now, I would lose control and all I really wanted to do was strangle her.

Instead, I decided to go find someone I could trust to help me. I didn't know how he would react, but I braced myself before I knocked on his door.

I heard a growl before the door opened and I made sure my hands were visible and raised in surrender.

"It's just me Dave. Something's happened and I need someone to talk to.

His nostrils were flaring as he stood in the doorway glaring at me. I knew then that my assumptions were correct, I smelled like demon.

I kept my breathing slow and steady as he watched me silently. "I just need to talk to clear my mind, because if I don't I'm either going to do something stupid or walk into a trap."

He opened the door and stood to the side so I could enter. "I should have stayed away from her... You told me from the start that she was trouble, but I never imagined this. Then she showed up in my class and I just couldn't stay away... and now I know she's been working for them the whole time."

"Who? Jacki?" He looked surprised as he shut the door behind me

"Yes, Jacki. That bitch has been working for demons. She's got a fucking demon mark tattoo on her arm. It broke my mother's majik, she called me frantic thinking I was dead. I've got demons coming for me and I don't know what to do, but all I want to do is go wring her fucking neck."

"Hold on a minute," he pulled out his phone

and made a call.

"Hey T, remember back when you told me about that weird dream Jax had?" There was a pause as she answered and he continued, "I was trying to tell Jules about it, but I know I'll screw it up. I'm gonna put you on speaker, he doesn't believe me when I say she's bat shit crazy."

He pressed the speaker button and held the phone out between us.

"It's not that she's crazy, I think she just has a big imagination, ya know?" She laughed before going on. "Okay, so she showed up at work one day freaking out about this tattoo on her arm. She swore some crazy monster put it there, like, she had a dream about this dude slaughtering these people and then supposedly woke up to find the same dude in her apartment. He grabbed her arm and the tattoo showed up.

"I told her she was nuts, like that kind of shit doesn't actually happen, it's just weird fucking scary movie crap. So I told her she probably just got blackout drunk and hallucinated the whole thing, but she kept going on about the tattoo.

"She probably got it while she was drunk and just didn't remember, but she swore it wasn't a tattoo and wasn't there the day before, and it wouldn't be that perfectly healed if it were that fresh."

I cut her off, "Did she say why the guy gave her the tattoo? What did it look like?"

"It was just a crazy dream Julius, but I don't know. She said something about he wanted her to find someone but never told her anymore details, so it doesn't make any sense. It had to have just been a dream, it was too fucking weird, so maybe she is nuts? I mean maybe that's why she's always moving around, people find out she's psycho and she has to leave."

"Tera, what did the tattoo look like?" I hated that I had to ask her again, but she was kind of flaky.

"Ugh," she let out a frustrated sound, "it's that weird symbol on her arm, with the random letters. I know you've seen it, she got it like the day before y'all met."

Dave cut in before she could say any more, "Thank you Tera! I tried to tell him she was crazy, but he wouldn't believe me. Gotta go though, we're at the gym."

"Mmmkay, bye Davie!"

I raised an eyebrow at his lie as he shoved the phone back into his pocket.

"I did that because Jacki has never had any demon scent. If she was working with them, she would have a faint smell, but this seems off. There hasn't been any demon activity lately, at least not since your last incident."

None of it made sense. If Tera's story about Jacki was true, then she had no idea what was even going on. I still wanted to confront her, but I didn't think I could keep a cool head long enough to do so.

As if he could read my thoughts, Dave spoke up. "I don't think it's wise for you to go see her, especially being this pissed off at her. Plus it could be a trap, I'll call a couple hunters to go check it out."

I took a deep breath, grateful that I had made a friend with supernatural ties and understood the parts of myself that I didn't quite understand myself.

I'd learned more about hunters from Dave than my mother had ever cared to mention. She had wanted to protect me, but her idea of protection involved keeping me ignorant. The less I knew, the safer I would be in her eyes.

I thought otherwise, knowing that I could protect myself better if I knew what I was up against.

I'd started my research in my teens, but didn't realize how little I actually knew until I'd met Dave. He'd introduced me to the idea of the hunters, typically made up of different types of supes but they were primarily human.

They mostly went after demons, but any supernatural creature that got out of line usually found themselves on the wrong side of the hunters.

"I'm gonna call it in," he picked up an Xbox controller and tossed it at me, "sit tight, we'll play a few rounds till you cool off."

As much as I didn't care for videogames, I still loaded it up and set up a profile to play a few practice rounds while he made his phone call. I tried not to listen to him, trying to focus on the game instead but I couldn't help but eavesdrop.

"Hey, it's Ward. I've got a lead on possible activity, I need a few of you to head over to

9812 Linwood on the Indy side to check it out. It might be a trap or nothing at all, just scope it out and let me know what you find." His voice dropped low as he took a few more steps away, "There might be a girl there, and I don't know how involved she is but try to keep her alive."

Try to keep her alive, ha. I focused my attention back to the TV. Funny how last week I couldn't get enough of her and today I was ready to see her dead.

Dave had told me from the start that she was bad news, but in the most innocent of ways. I didn't need someone in my life that would up and vanish one day, but I didn't want anyone to get close to me either. She was the ultimate danger. Knowing she wouldn't be around forever made me want her all the more. I wanted to share my secrets and my fears with her but that was my downfall.

She was a weapon against me and someone had known it from the start. My days of hiding from my own blood were over, the demons were pushing me out into the light and a deep dark part of me was grateful.

I started a new game and focused on it to tune him out until a beer was placed in front of me and he joined in.

We played a few rounds before his phone started ringing. He answered and propped it between his shoulder and ear while continuing to play.

"Yeah?" He listened for a moment before

dropping the controller and jumping to his feet. "How bad?"

I gave up on the game and shut off his Xbox. Dave was deathly quiet as a voice was almost yelling through the speaker.

I chugged my beer and wondered what was being said before Dave put the call on speaker and held it out between us again.

"…two demons, had to have been royal guards. They were powerful and trashing the place."

Dave cut him off, "What about the girl?"

"That fucker Maxx took her through a portal right as we got there. I don't know how she got involved or who she is, but they have her."

"Did it look willing or was she actually taken?"

"I don't think it was willing, she was unconscious and had a bloody lip. She must have put up a fight. The demons were no good for answers, they were trashing the place and teleported out before we got a chance to do any damage to them."

The man on the phone took in a deep breath, "This is fucked up man, the closest we've gotten to Maxx in months and he was here on our home turf. The fucker is just toying with us now. How did you know he would be here?"

Dave spared a glance at me and I answered the guy. "She had his mark tattooed on her arm and it flared to life and knocked me on my ass earlier."

"How long has she had the tattoo? How

long have you known her?"

Dave cut back in, "Are you sure it was Maxx that took her through the portal?"

"Oh yeah, it was definitely him.   I'm sorry man, but there's not much more I can tell you.   He took the girl and his guards left just as quick, not even bothering to rough any of us up."

Dave sighed, "Thank you Miller, let me know if anything else happens."   He hung up and looked at me.

"How much do you know about the other realms besides earth?"

I didn't know jack shit about any other realms.   In prior years I'd managed to get a few drunks to talk about other worlds, but since they were drunk I didn't assume them to be very credible, plus anyone with any sense wouldn't spill details to an ordinary human.

"Not much, no one talks about secrets when they assume you're human."

Dave nodded, "Fair enough.   Essentially, Earth Realm has been the original neutral ground. The people here are typically non-majik species, just your ordinary humans.   The other realms are where your supes originated from.   Faeries, demons, witches, vamps, weres and shifters all have homes.   Most of the other realms are pretty mixed now but they're still fairly segregated as far as the interactions go.

"The only way to access any of these other realms is by using a portal.   Like earth, they're all big places divided into colonies or cities, but with a single ruler in charge of that realm. Most have royal families with the heir taking over when the previous king or queen steps down or dies.

"There's always the occasional war, certain realms a little more unsteady than the others. Every once in a while you have the supes that come to earth to start over somewhere new, families that start here and down the line you have weres like me who have only ever known Earth Realm and don't feel any loyalty to their original lineage."

He reached down and took a swig of his beer, "A lot of the legend and lore that you're familiar with here actually all stems from these other realms, especially the demons and the Haelexii realm. Their current ruler, Maxx Solomon is a real sonuvabitch. He's been causing quite a bit of chaos here lately, and based on what's happening with Jacki I'd say he's targeting you for a reason.

"If this demon is your father and people find out, you're going to be on everyone's most wanted list pretty quick."

His voice trailed off and he looked at me then, "We're friends Jules, but if you go darkside I'm not sure what kind of advice I can give you. I've worked hard to stay neutral in all of this."

I knew I had a ruthless side, but to be made aware that my blood was evil and I had little to no chance of ignoring it any longer? It was a tough pill to swallow. I only hoped I didn't lose sight of my humanity.

"Thank you David, for everything. I'm not

going to drag you any further into this."   I turned to go and he reached out and put a hand on my shoulder.

"If you ever need any help, you know where to find me.   Just try to keep a cool head man and don't do anything crazy."

I nodded and stepped out the door.

Crazy?   That wouldn't even begin to cover what I was planning to do. I just had to hurry because there was a chance my mother was already on her way to check on me.

Chapter Nine

*** Julius ***

I was standing in my kitchen as I wrapped my hand around the knife blade and pulled it through. My teeth were gritted as I held in a hiss of pain and let the blood drip into a bowl. I had no idea if this would work, but it was worth a shot.

I knew from my mother that blood majik was one of the most powerful types and now that the demon side of myself was free I swore I could feel the energy coursing through each drop that spilled out of me.

I wrapped a bandage around the cut hand and picked up my phone to look at the symbol again.

I had a small paintbrush ready as I used the blood to draw the symbol onto the countertop. With each line I drew, the air felt thicker and a slight buzzing noise formed in my ears as I came closer to finishing.

I looked at the picture one last time to put the final pieces down, the energy almost suffocating me as it filled the room. The moment the symbol was finished it burst into flame and burned into the counter making it permanent. The buzzing noise in my ears grew louder as the symbol glowed red.

By some unknown instinct I dipped my uncut hand into the last of the blood and slammed my palm down onto the center of the symbol while shouting, "Maxx you fucker! If you want me, then come get me!"

A bright white light blasted up from around my hand but I held steady and pushed back against the force.   I put all of my weight into it as the light tried to force me back.   It lasted only a few seconds before the light died down and all the majik I had felt earlier vanished from the room.

"That was quite impressive.   Something mommy taught you?"

I turned towards the voice behind me, "No, I learned that all on my own."

I don't know what I was expecting but he looked...normal.   Clean cut and taller than myself with the same short brown hair.   A plain black t-shirt and jeans, he could have been my older brother but didn't look old enough to be my father.   He couldn't have been forty yet, but I knew from research that different species tended to age differently.

"What do you want with me?"   My arms crossed my chest and I leaned back against the counter.   I was much calmer than I should have been, but that was a good thing, right?

"Do you want the bullshit answer, or the truth?"   His pose mimicked mine as he leaned against the door frame.

"If you're just going to bullshit me then you can go ahead and leave.   I thought whatever it was would be important enough to justify using an innocent woman against me."

"Oh, Jacki?! Isn't she delightful?" He smiled, "She has power that she doesn't even know about and will never realize her full potential without a little help. I knew she'd attract you, I just didn't realize how close you would get."

He uncrossed his arms and leaned against the door frame. "You know, the little bitch refused to give you up once she realized who you were? It was almost sweet, but you and I both know it was too late by then. The moment you touched my mark I could find you on my own."

"Why were you suddenly so apt to find me? I'm almost thirty." If I pushed about Jacki right now I would lose my calm, so I tried changing the subject slightly.

"YOU are my rightful heir and could potentially harness more power than any other demon in existence. No one would be able to challenge you for the throne with that kind of power... I just didn't realize your mother was serious when she vowed to never let any child of hers become a demon. I suppose I was quite a bit of a deceitful asshole back then, parading about as a witch, I must have broken her heart when she learned the truth."

"I don't care about your stories." I cut him off and his eyes flashed red at me. "All I want to know is what you want from me."

He was silent a while as he sized me up. "I want you, plain and simple. Come to Hael Realm, embrace your demon blood and learn from me.   If you progress as well as I hope, then I want you in line for the seat of power you deserve."

"When?"

"Ten years ago would have been nice, but I'll take you today if it's my only option."

"I'll agree... Conditionally."

He raised a brow at me, baffled that it could be so easy to convince me.

"I have a life here that I can't just up and leave."   I held up a finger to silence him as I continued.   "You can have me until Sunday, but then I have classes to teach.   You work around MY schedule until I say otherwise."

"Done."

"Also, Jacki is out.   She doesn't need involved any longer.   I want the mark removed and for her to be off limits to all demon kind."

"She's not ever going to be the same, you should know that.   A prisoner never forgets their captor or the reasoning behind their sentence."

"She'll overcome it, but I want her released first."

"On Sunday when you return, you can bring her back."

"I want her returned NOW."   I was struggling to control my temper.

"Sunday."

"I'm not going to back out on our deal Maxx."

"Neither am I, but what do you plan to do when your mother shows up to find her here and you gone away?"

Shit, I had forgotten about my mother. It had been hours since her frantic calls thinking me dead.

"Teach me to mask the demon smell and power. If I can convince her that everything is fine, then we'll both have peace. If she knows I'm with you, she'll stop at nothing to find me and destroy you in the process."

His care free mask fell for a brief moment as my words sank in, then just as quickly it was gone.

"No. When she arrives you will tell her your choice. You are going to accompany me willingly and she will have to accept it. It will break her but it is nothing she hasn't dealt with before."

I suddenly wondered about my mother and how exactly she had gotten mixed up with Maxx in the first place. She had always seemed so strong but I had to wonder just how broken she truly was.

"Fine. Sunday." I picked up my phone and pulled up my contacts list. "But we're leaving now."

She answered on the first ring. "Jules! I'm so glad you called! I tried to book a flight to come visit but everything is overbooked with the holiday and I can't get out until tomorrow."

"Mom," my voice held steady, "it's okay, and I'm fine. The girl just tasered me, no majik. It was my fault for being too handsy. I'm actually not even home right now, Dave talked me into going with him to a family lake house to get away from the girls."

"I don't think it's safe for you to be going out right now Jules."

"He's a hunter, I trust him with my life. If anything happens I'm in good hands, plus he said I'm not registering any different, just ordinary human."

The lies just kept rolling out of my mouth and Maxx cleared his throat and tapped his watch.

"I'm probably going to lose signal soon, we're already two hours past city limits. I'll call you Monday after class"

"I love you Julius...be safe." Her words were a whisper and if felt like she could see through my lies.

"Love you too Ma." I ended the call and shut the phone back off, plugging it into the charger and leaving it on the counter.

"If you lie that easily to your own mother, I can only imagine the respect you'll have for me."

"Let's just get this over with." I didn't want to stand around discussing my mother with him.

He extended his hand as if to shake on a deal and I took it without thought. The moment my skin touched his I felt the energy buzz through me and my eyes blinked closed at the noise.

In that one quick blink everything changed. We were no longer in my kitchen, but another house completely.

"That was teleportation, a very simple trick. We're in one of my homes on Earth Realm now. I have a permanent portal here." He had already released my hand and was taking a few steps down the hallway.

He stopped at a door leading outside and turned to me. "First lesson, open this door."

I gave him a sidelong glance as I paused before reaching for the handle. It opened with ease and revealed a spacious driveway with a large wall surrounding the property.

In the distance it looked like the Forbidden City. "Are we in China?"

"Yes, and still Earth Realm. Close the door and try again."

I shut the door and opened it again, knowing it would be the same thing. When it was I slammed the door and turned to face him. "Is this a joke?"

"Do you know how many times you've touched a portal but it was useless to you because you didn't know any better?"

He reached past me and opened the door again. This time it wasn't China, but a jungle of some sort. We stepped out and I looked around as best I could. Three suns burned in the sky and the sweat was already dripping down my spine. We were on a mountain with miles of jungle all around.

I turned back around toward the door and realized even it had changed. It wasn't the small entry door like you'd see on a typical house, nor was it a house. It was a stone castle and the door was at least twelve feet high of solid wood.

An explosion grabbed my attention and I

turned back toward the jungle to witness a volcano erupting in the distance.

"Ahh, dinner time, come on."

He pushed the oversized wooden door open with ease and into the castle we went.

Just ten minutes ago I had been at home in Kansas City. Then I'd visited Beijing China, and now I was in a completely different world altogether.

"Welcome to Haelexii Julius," Maxx called over his shoulder. "I do hope you enjoy your new home."

Chapter Ten

** *Jacki* **

My eyes fluttered open and nothing looked familiar. *Where am I?* The last thing I remembered was being held by the demons, beaten and bloodied.

I pushed the covers down off my body and looked myself over. No cuts, bruises or blood. I was exceptionally clean, with a fresh tank top and panties.

I sat up and examined my arm. The mark was gone. A little voice in the back of my mind told me that it wasn't real, that this was just another dream and I would wake up to still being tortured.

I stretched and got out of the bed, my body achy from phantom bruises. I went into an adjoining bathroom and looked into the mirror. I looked remarkably healthy, not what was expected of someone who had spent days being a tortured prisoner.

I used the toilet and saw a pile of clothes laid out for me. I pulled on the jeans and sweater and slipped into the tennis shoes before quietly opening the door and looking into the hallway.

I knew exactly where I was then, I had just never been in the spare room.

I walked down the hall to find Julius sitting at his kitchen table with a cup of coffee grading papers. The floors creaked under my steps as I approached and his gaze drifted up to look at me.

He almost looked sad as he asked, "Are you hungry?"

"Am I really here?" My voice cracked and I winced at it.

"Yes, you're here. I took care of everything and you're safe now. I'm sorry you were involved in Maxx's petty games." He was calm as he spoke and it made me want to hit him.

"How?"

A shadow crossed his face as he shuffled some papers together and stood. "My mother was honest with me most of my life, I knew she was a witch and I knew my father was a demon that would eventually come looking for me. I just never expected to meet you."

His hand cupped my face and he gave me a gentle kiss before turning away. "The mark is gone and you should be safe from all demon kind now. Your house was pretty trashed, but I managed to get it cleaned up the best I could."

My mind was spinning. "I didn't know it was real Julius, I thought it was just a nightmare about a demon because of how my mom died... and I was drinking too much..." I choked on my own words, "...once I realized it was real, you touched the tattoo and it was too late. I could feel the power burning me and I knew I had to run...but he was waiting for me."

My mind flashed back to after Maxx had taken me and I fell to my knees as I remembered fighting for my life against three demons as Maxx stood and watched. *"You just have to agree to my terms Miss Donovan and this can stop."*

I would fight until darkness took me, then I would wake up healed and it would start all over again.

I started to hyperventilate thinking that this was just another ruse, any moment now Julius would vanish and I'd be alone with the demons again.

"Jacki!" Julius shook me back to myself until I looked up at him with tears streaming down my face. He pulled me up into his embrace and rubbed my back, "Shhh, it's going to be okay."

He let me cry a while and when my sniffles calmed down he spoke with his face buried in my hair. "I figured it out right after you left and got you out as soon as I could but there were conditions." One of his hands moved up to smooth my hair, "I'm dangerous to you, toxic. As long as you stay away from me you'll be safe; you'll be able to live a normal life, demon free."

He pushed me away just enough to look at my face. I stared into his eyes as he wiped away my tears and I wondered how I would be able to walk away from such a man.

But as he wiped my tears, I realized every single one was because of him, every invisible bruise I felt was his fault. If I didn't walk away now I would only hurt myself more in the long run.

I stared into his golden brown eyes and saw my own fear and sadness mirrored back at me, but I also saw the same determination that I felt.

I closed my eyes and kissed him then, pouring every emotion I had into our lips. If it was time to say goodbye then it I would make it one to remember.

As I slowly pulled away I couldn't bear to open my eyes and look at him. "Goodbye Julius." I turned away and opened my eyes to navigate down the hall and out the door.

He didn't stop me and it wasn't until I'd walked a few blocks into the Westport area that I started shivering and realized I didn't have any money or ID.

There was a line in front of the Riot Room and I just hoped Robbie was working or someone I knew would be inside to help me with a ride home. I waited in line and when the bouncer asked for the cover fee I didn't hesitate to open my mouth.

"Is Robbie bartending tonight?" I had no idea what day it was as I stood there shivering, "I just need to talk to him really quick."

He gave me one of those looks that told me he was instantly judging me as a crazy bitch.

"Dude, I'm serious. Tell him Jacki is out here and it's an emergency. I don't have my phone or wallet and I'm miles from home."

Someone behind me spoke up. "She's here all the time RJ, don't be a dick. I'll pay." A pale freckled hand reached past me and gave the bouncer a couple bills and then put his arms on my shoulders to steer me inside.

I turned to see if my assumptions were correct and saw that it was Dave with a guitar case slung over his shoulder.

"Thank you," I muttered before dropping my head and trying to shrug away.

I glanced toward the bar to look for Robbie, but Dave kept his hold on my shoulders and leaned down to whisper in my ear. "We need to talk Jax."

"I'm not really in the mood." I tried to pull away again but he spun me around to face him.

"Three days ago you were taken by demons and now you're walking around here like it was no big deal. How did you get back?"

How did he even know about what happened? I knew he was close friends with Julius, but this seemed unreal. I didn't know how to answer him and I nervously pulled the sweater tighter around myself as I shivered.

He sighed and hugged me close, becoming my own heating blanket. "If there is anyone in this city that you can trust and talk to about this, it's me. I'm not your average human and I know a lot more than I let on. I just need to know how you got back to earth or I'm going to have to call some hunters to keep an eye on you until we know you're not some kind of walking trap."

I pushed away from him and pulled up my right sleeve. "The mark is gone. I don't know how he did it, but Julius said he made a deal to save me and I woke up at his house maybe an hour ago."

I was on the verge of crying again as I

pulled the sleeve back down, "He said I'd be safe as long as I stay away from him, so I left… but I don't have my car or wallet or phone. I don't even know what day it is. I just want to go home and try not to cry anymore until I can figure out what to do."

He hugged me again, "I'm sorry Jax, and life's a bitch sometimes. I can take you home, I just gotta drop off this guitar with Bobby. It's Sunday night by the way."

I looked toward the bar again but there was a different bartender working and no one in the crowd looked familiar. "Yes please, that would be great." I finally answered.

He peeled off his jacket and handed it to me, "Here, put this on, I'm going to go take this backstage." He walked away quickly and was back almost as fast to lead me back outside to his truck parked a block away.

He cranked the heat up and didn't say a word until we were in my driveway. He had been to my house several times before when Tera would leave her car at my house for a night out, so I didn't think twice about him knowing exactly how to get there.

I was happy to see my van still in the driveway as I shrugged back out of Dave's coat and set it on the seat between us.

"Did he say how he got you out?"

I turned and looked at him, and even though we weren't very close I could tell he was worried. Getting mixed up with demons was something I'd never expected, even with my fascination with the paranormal I had never really believed any of it to actually be real.   Yet I'd spent the weekend as a prisoner by a demon king and had some serious emotional attachment to his son.

I knew the only way Maxx would have let me go was if Julius gave into his demon side.   I had seen the darkness behind his eyes before I said goodbye.

Could I admit it aloud and face the truth right now?   I didn't know what Dave was or how much he really knew, but I knew I wasn't ready for their world.

"I don't know Dave but if I can put the pieces together I'm sure you can too.   I won't be seeing him again, I know that much."

I opened the door and let the frigid winter wind numb me as I jumped down to the ground and typed in my garage code to go inside. I had to stop and look around to be sure I was in the right house.

All of my furniture was gone and replaced with new items.   I found my phone and wallet both in the pockets of the coat I had been wearing before I was taken.

I went to my room to find the phone charger and plugged it in.   It was definitely dead so I walked away and went to shower.   Maybe it would help clear my head.

I put on a fresh tank top and shorts and curled up on my couch to start a Netflix binge.   I didn't know how to cope with these feelings and all I really wanted to do was pack up my van and leave.

I put on a show with about ten seasons

available and let my brain go numb as it continued to play episode after episode. I'm not sure how many episodes I watched before I fell asleep.

I woke up Monday and had pizza delivered, staying on the couch and continuing to watch show after show. Sometime Tuesday afternoon I'd made up my mind and sent a text to an old friend from the road.

Me- I hope you're somewhere warm, I'm looking to rage it!

If he was still a traveler I had no doubt that he would be somewhere nice and welcome me to join.

I looked around at all of my things and started making calls to utility companies. I wasn't going to permanently leave, so I planned on make sure everything here was kept in order so I would have a home to come back to.

I didn't bother reading all the texts I had from Tera. Apparently Dave mentioned to her that Julius and I had broken up and her calls had been almost nonstop. I didn't bother arguing that we weren't even dating to begin with, but eventually I sent her a message saying it had been mutual and I was fine. She was at work today so the calls and texts had stopped for a little bit.

I cleaned out my fridge and cabinets of anything that might go bad while I was away. It didn't take very long so soon I was throwing a few things into a small backpack. My phone had chimed at some point and it was after ten pm when I finally read the text.

Tommy- Rainbow starts next week. Chiapas Mexico.

I smiled knowing I didn't need to reply. With those six words he knew I would be there regardless of what was going on.

Tommy was one of the first street kids that I met years ago on Venice Beach. Originally from Chicago he felt the call of the road in his teens and had been traveling ever since. He was more of a hippie than anything else and the rainbow gathering was exactly where I would have guessed he would be.

Nothing says peace and love like a few hundred hippies in the forest somewhere.

I looked up Chiapas Mexico and my smile grew brighter. There was a jungle right along the Mexico and Guatemala border that I knew the gathering would be. It wouldn't be too hot since it was December, but it would be nice tropical weather.

I looked up flights and booked the first one that would get me somewhat close to where I needed to go. I'd be leaving as early as six am.

I changed into more appropriate clothes and a light hoodie for the trip down. It may be nice down in the jungle, but it was still cold here.

I phoned a cab and while waiting I went to the school's website and dropped my classes.

Right as a horn honked from my driveway I updated my Facebook status and grabbed my bag to run out the door.

"Fuck winter, see you guys at Rainbow"

Chapter Eleven

** *Jacki* **

There was a small town just outside the Villahermosa airport and after a twenty minute walk I stopped to get something to eat from a little corner taqueria. My Spanish wasn't great but it was enough to get by.

I got directions to the only gas station in town near the highway and as luck would have it a microbus of hippies pulled up just as I was walking in.

"Hey!" I said, jogging up to meet them as they all got out. None of them looked familiar but that didn't mean anything. The driver had the stereotypical tie-dye grateful dead shirt with a flowing skirt and dreadlocks. He was like the poster child for hippies.

"Are you all heading to the gathering?" It was an obvious question but there was always the chance that it was a coincidence to run into fellow travelers in an unfamiliar place.

"Yeah man, we're still about five hours out. Gotta get down towards the Bonampak ruins, you need a ride sister?" He wiped his hands on his skirt as he opened the cap to the fuel tank.

"I would appreciate one and I can even buy this tank of fuel for you."

His face brightened with a smile and he reached out and pulled me in for a hug pressing my face into his brown dreads. "My name is Peter, welcome home!" I hugged back as I tried not to react to his sweaty smell. A few more days and I'd smell the same.

Welcome home was the typical greeting at a gathering and it lifted my spirits already. "I'm Jax," I replied, Dave's nickname slipping out before I could say anything else.

The five others all came up and introduced themselves and before too long everyone was climbing back in as I went to pay the attendant and we got on the road.

It had been years since I last attended a gathering and I was ready for the love and acceptance it brought. I stayed with Peter and his group for about a day before I got recruited into the kitchen setup.

They were part of the early setup group and I did what I could to help out as more people started to slowly trickle in.

By the sixth day there were already a hundred people on site and finally I ran into my friend Tommy. He had been spending time up in the Portland Oregon area with some girl and Rainbow Gathering was his chance to get away and breathe a bit. It was really good seeing him and a few others that I had known throughout the years on the streets.

As the days went on we became familiar with the jungle and the nearby ruins. We would take walks over to the ruins and lay out in the sun, or swim in the nearby rivers or lakes. Everything was a bit of a walk from the campsite, but it was a beautiful place.

There were drum circles around campfires at night, with the occasional wooden flute or didgeridoo player joining in as well as we all sang and danced together.

It was a great distraction while I was awake, but all bets were off when I slept. My subconscious must have wanted to see him again because the nightmares began again of Maxx and his exploits.

I knew better than to react, instead I would silently turn and walk away begging myself to wake up. Some nights when Julius was with him I would watch a while before turning to go, but I never stayed for long.

I don't think either knew I was able to watch and I prayed that they never found out. I had been in the jungle for three weeks when I took an afternoon nap up against a tree. The dream hit not long after I fell asleep and it shook me to my core. I recognized the surroundings instantly, having spent many days at the Bonampak ruins in the previous weeks.

It was a battleground as the sun was setting in the distance and I held in a terrified cry as I saw the chaos of men and women fighting. Some had eyes glowing red and I knew they were demons, and others I was unsure of.

I turned to run back to camp, hoping to wake myself up as I saw Maxx trapped in some kind of force field atop the taller ruin.

Usually when I was dreaming I knew my energy was dispersed and my physical form wasn't actually there. I shouldn't have been able to run into someone, but I did. I hadn't been paying attention as I knocked the man to the ground and a look of confusion crossed his face as he recognized me. It was the buff tattooed man I had seen fighting Maxx the first time I saw him in my dreams.

I was just as shocked as recognition struck but before he could react I woke up gasping exactly where I had settled down at camp. It couldn't have been the same man, could it? I had watched him take several bullets to the chest, I saw him die.

I grabbed my backpack and shoved my few things into it where I had them hanging to dry. The sun was still setting as I jumped to my feet and started heading towards the ruins. If the dreams were as real as the demon had first said, then I was going to find out.

Once I was away from the campsite and in the jungle I started to run. I heard someone call out my name but I didn't stop to chat. I had to know.

My pace slowed as I fought my way off the path to get there faster. I was in the jungle so I probably shouldn't have been out alone let alone off the path, but as I saw a cloud of smoke through the dense trees I pressed on faster.

A jaguar jumped into my path forcing me to stop just before the clearing. I froze only a moment before speaking to it. "Get the fuck out of my way."

It was stupid of me, but it was my first reaction. The thing was probably going to kill me, but instead the cat simply looked at me a moment before darting back into the brush and running off.

It was bizarre yet I didn't dwell on it.

I emerged into the clearing in time to see Maxx snapping a man's neck. Julius stood beside him with his arms crossed as if he was bored by the scene. Neither of them looked my way as I strode towards them.

The ground was littered with bodies and the foliage past the clearing was ablaze. Some of the bodies were fellow travelers, some looked like locals.

"You son of a bitch!" I shouted at Maxx as I grew closer.

Their heads shot in my direction and Julius looked very shocked to see me. Maxx smiled and gave a half bow as he grabbed hold of his son's arm and they both vanished.

I had only a moment to process the situation before I was surrounded by four men with their guns drawn. The one that I had seen several times before and tackled earlier was the first to speak.

"Who are you and why are you here?"

I slowly raised my hands up and looked around. "My name is Jacki Donovan and I'm camping nearby. I saw the smoke…" My words trailed off as I wondered how to really answer them.

The guns pointed at me made me hesitate from lying, but I didn't think I could tell the truth either.

The sun had set, but the blaze from the forest fire gave enough light to see a very large and very naked dark skinned man approach us. His voice was thick with the local Spanish accent.

"She is human but somehow marked as off limits to the demons. There was a group she passed in the jungle and they didn't even attempt to touch her. I managed to get one to speak before ripping out his throat."

My mouth stayed shut as I remembered the last conversation I had with Julius.

The man continues, "They say she is protected by the King's law." He approached me, pushing one of the men's guns aside to look down into my face. "She was not scared of my animal form."

A thousand thoughts passed through my mind, but as I swallowed back my own fear I saw the answer in his eyes as he stared down at me. The jaguar in my path had been this man. Demons existed, so why not shifters?

"What was your rush to be here?"

Even though he was nude and the only one that didn't have a gun pointed at me, I knew he was the deadliest of the five men.

"I knew Maxx was here, I had to prove I was right and see for myself."

Another man came running up before anyone could acknowledge my answer. "We need to get out of here before more civilians show up because of the fire. The demons have all gone."

I looked at the bodies littered around and my heart broke. Three of the men dropped their guns from aiming at me, and slung them over their shoulders to go drag several bodies into the fire that was already spreading rapidly.

"You and I have more to talk about, so don't even think about going anywhere." It was the man from before.

"You can put your gun away, I'm not a threat. I'm hoping you can give me answers too since I keep running into you."

The naked shifter stepped away and turned to the aggressive bald one. "I must return to the village and keep my people away." I must have blinked because instead of a man walking away, the jaguar was bounding back into the jungle.

I stared a little too long because the other man cleared his throat. "You don't seem very surprised at that trick, but you must not be used to it."

I turned back to him, "I've been learning how real nightmares can be, especially since I am in the jungle talking to you while surrounded by dead bodies. It's been a pretty fucking weird year, and it's a long story, so if you plan on keeping me hostage we should probably get a move on."

He seemed a little surprised at my declaration and reached to grab my arm.

I yanked away before he could and took a step back. "Not a demon are ya?"

He blinked and laughed at me before he sobered up and realized I was being serious. "No, I'm not a demon, I'm a hunter. My name's Calvin."

He must have realized just how clueless I was at that point because he studied me a while longer as I nodded and said "Okay."

"There's a truck over by the road, c'mon." He turned and jogged in that direction trusting me to follow, and I did.

If my weeks in the jungle taught me anything, it was that there was no way I could avoid this world now. I was too curious to just forget everything I had been through.

Dave had offered to help me before I left KC, even mentioning the hunters once or twice but I hadn't quite decided what I was going to do at that point. Right now though, I was going to learn all that I could, even if that meant I'd be joining the hunters to try and kill Maxx. If that's what they were even trying to do.

I jogged after Calvin and climbed into the cab with him as the other men all jumped into the bed and we took off down the dirt road away from the ruins.

Chapter Twelve

** *Julius* **

"You promised me she would be safe!" My finger shoved into Maxx's face.

He brushed my hand away as if I were nothing but an annoying fly buzzing about. The moment Jacki had appeared in the jungle he had teleported us away.

She had looked wild and I had to wonder if she had been among that group that attacked us outside the portal.

The hunters had somehow found one of the major portals used by the Haelexii Demons and had a trap waiting when we arrived. They were prepared for demons and hoped for Maxx, but they hadn't anticipated me.

Even though I was part demon, I was still half witch. I had easily stepped out of the spell and teleported behind the spell caster and snapped his neck.

The act should have ate at my conscious, but I had been spending the past month with some of the vilest demons in existence, the ones nightmares were based off of. The moment Maxx was free he summoned a dozen of his guard to the site, bringing fire to the jungle as they fought the hunters.

Several of the demons died in the fight but the hunters scattered as their numbers also faltered.

"Leave my portals alone!" Maxx had shouted at a group of hunters with guns trained on him. I was by his side as he waved his hand and the hunters were all thrown back except one.

I crossed my arms as I watched my father snap his neck without a second thought, and that's when Jacki had shouted from the clearing.

"You son of a bitch!"

Right as I was about to teleport to her side, Maxx took my arm and we were gone. I looked around and realized he had brought us to my own home back in Kansas City.

"She IS safe—from demons. How was I to know she would be camping with jungle peasants near one of my portals?" He took a step away from me and hopped up to sit on my kitchen table. "It was only a matter of time before she found the hunters anyway."

"She was in a fucking jungle in Mexico that is always overflowing with demons, how is that safe?!" I was pissed. I had made a deal with Maxx, Jacki's safety and freedom for my own.

"Honestly Julius, surrounded by demons is the safest place she can be. If any of them were to even try to harm her they would pay the ultimate price. They can't touch her."

The walls and floors of my home were trembling as my emotions overpowered my control and turned to wild majik. I took a deep breath to calm myself and waited for the ground to steady.

"Is she working with the hunters?"

He jumped back off the table and looked at me knowing I would want his eye contact to whatever answer he gave. "She wasn't with them before today, but I can assume she is with them now. Especially when that angry bald one realizes he's seen her before."

I ignored his coaxing, "Will they hurt her?"

"No." He was very quick to respond. "Hunters are a strange breed, but they are naturally protective. Once they know she's not a threat she will be accepted. Given what she knows of you and her hatred for me, I can only assume she'll start training soon." He started laughing, "A hunter that can't be touched by a demon. She'll make rank pretty quickly I imagine."

I let it all sink in for a moment before I turned to the kitchen counter where his symbol was permanently seared into the marble. "I'll come back to Haelexii tomorrow, but I need you to leave now."

I summoned my majik as quickly and silently as I could while pouring it out through my hand as I slammed my palm into the symbol. The white noise pounded through my head a brief moment and with a flash of light the majik pulsed outward and Maxx was forced off earth realm.

It was a trick he didn't know I had mastered, and he would be pissed the next time I saw him, but he deserved it.

I was finally alone in my home as I went and

powered on my laptop. I went to Jacki's Facebook page and saw her tagged in several photos in the jungle, always with a group of hippies and all captioned with "Rainbow Gathering!" I scrolled down to find the last time she posted and it was just a simple status. *"Fuck winter, see you guys at Rainbow"*

I opened google and searched for "rainbow gathering in Mexico" and found a database for hippie gatherings. As far as I could tell Maxx was right. Her being in the same area was nothing but a coincidence.

I went to Dave's page next and saw a post from an hour ago talking about a show he was playing tonight. I looked at the time, almost eight pm. I shut the computer back off and almost made it out the door before I caught my reflection in a mirror.

I was filthy. My hair and beard was grown out of control and my clothes were splattered in blood. I sighed as I turned back around and went to go clean up. I could shower and shave, but my hair would just have to be ignored for now.

I hadn't seen or spoken to Dave since the day Jacki had been taken. I had resigned from my job at the school and left the Monday after I got back from Haelexii. I had told Maxx I would retain my life here, but in just the few short days I spent with him, I knew I couldn't go back to my life.

I'm sure Dave knew exactly why I disappeared so soon and I knew that meeting him wouldn't go over very well, but it was something I had to do.

Before I left the house I grabbed a watch I had spelled a few days earlier. As long as I didn't try to channel any demon majik while wearing it, it would mask the demon scent and allow me to pass for human.

I had already walked the several blocks to Westport before someone said, "Aren't you fuckin' cold buddy?" I realized my mistake immediately. I didn't have a coat on and was walking through several inches of snow. I'd gotten so used to regulating my body temperature in all the different climates that it had become second nature. I dropped the majik and allowed myself to feel the cold for the last few blocks.

There was no line outside tonight as I opened the door and entered the club. Dave's band was already playing as I paid the bouncer and joined the small crowd.

I had to wonder what day it was exactly because of how sparse the crowd really was. This was a place that was always filled no matter the night.

Dave's eyes were closed as he played a soft and smooth ballad on an acoustic guitar. When his eyes opened they locked right onto me. He continued to stare as he finished the tune, looking away only when he approached the microphone to address everyone else.

"We've got one last song and then Paul Bunyan's Bitch will take the stage. I really appreciate all of you guys coming out tonight. Merry Christmas!" He stepped back to switch to his electric guitar and the band broke out into one of their number one songs.

I cheered and sang along until it ended, feeling normal again for just a short while. As the crowd dispersed to go outside for a smoke or to the bar for drinks I snagged a table in the corner and waited.

The next band was on stage setting up when a pitcher of beer and two glasses were set on my table. I looked up at Dave as he filled both glasses and pushed one towards me. He had a poker face on as he studied me, and I saw the slight flare of his nostrils as he tried to pick up my scent.

"I know you're still a hunter Dave." The words spilled out before I could stop myself.

He took a drink, "And you're a demon prince."

"Jacki…" My words were caught in my throat and I reached for the beer.

"She left town the same time you did. She was pretty upset when you told her to get lost."

"I didn't…"

He cut me off. "You made some kind of deal to save her ass, I get it. But you gotta try and imagine what she went through, and the fact that you two had been getting close. You told her to stay away so she did what she does best and went on the road."

"To a Mexican Jungle?" This time my words silenced him. "She left here and went to the

Lacandon Jungle. She's been at some hippie camp right outside the Bonampak Ruins."

"Why would she go there?"

"You're the one that told me she was a drifter, that's what she does and that's just where she ended up. But today she showed up during that little raid or trap or whatever you want to call that shit the hunters did. Maxx teleported me away before I could even speak to her, and the hunters probably have her now."

"What do you want me to do?"

"Whatever you can to keep her safe. Vouch for her, anything you need to do. I didn't make a deal to protect her from the demons just to have some other species hurt her."

He took another drink of his beer and sat in silence a moment before answering me. "I'll help her as much as I can, but you have to know that she's the perfect example of how the hunters recruit. She's got a lot of reasons to hate demons."

"I know Dave, I know." We drank our beer in silence as the band started their first song.

After a little while he leaned towards me and spoke near my ear. "I need to ask you something Julius and I need you to be completely honest with me."

I paused before nodding and started to become uncomfortable.

"How many have you killed since I last saw you?"

My gut clenched and I couldn't answer. My mouth went dry stopping any words from having a chance of escape. I couldn't answer Dave, not because I was simply ashamed of the answer, but I honestly didn't know. In only a month's time I had lost count of all that I had murdered.

"That's what I thought." He got up and walked away leaving me silently suffocating.

I yanked the watch from my wrist and the air filled my lungs again as I teleported out of the club to my home.

I would never see my friend again because in that one silent moment I had transformed into the bad guy. The past month I had spent with Maxx I had been lying to myself, thinking I was still a good man inside, but Dave made sure I recognized my own evil.

The agony consumed me as my majik ran wild causing my house to become engulfed in flames. I stood in the center screaming until no more sound remained and the fire had consumed every inch of the home but the spot where I stood.

When I was certain there would be no saving it, I teleported to the nearest portal and left Earth realm.

I would no longer be calling it home.

Chapter Thirteen

** Jacki **

The drive to their base camp took a little over an hour. No one really knew what to do with me, but Calvin handed me a set of clothes and pointed me toward a bathroom.

"These should fit, we're flying back to the states here in about an hour or so, just gotta pick up some supplies." He went back out the door, barking orders into a walkie-talkie.

I changed and sat in a nearby chair with my mouth shut as I looked at all the security cameras trained all around the room. I had my passport in my hand as Calvin came back inside to fetch me.

"I was wondering if you had any sort of ID, but you won't be needing that." He took the book from my hand and looked at my information page a moment before flipping through the pages and looking at the stamps. "You get around huh? I didn't think you hippies had that kind of money."

He handed the passport back as I said, "I'm not a hippie."

He laughed, "Of course you aren't. You've just been in the jungle with them for a month. Let's go."

It was almost another hour to a local airport

where a private jet was waiting. We boarded and a man rushed up to Calvin with an urgent note just as they were about to seal the door. He scanned over it quickly, glancing my way before handing it back. "I'll call him when we land."

The man nodded as he turned and ran back off the plane as Calvin came and took the seat beside me.

The doors were shut and the plane started to taxi down the runway. "You should probably tell me how one of the commanders in Kansas City knows that we found you in the jungle and that you would be with me specifically."

"What?" The plane lurched to speed as I tried to think of how anyone would know where I was. Dave had mentioned hunters, but he didn't seem the badass killing type. If he was some commander, it would make sense that Julius would go to him after seeing me in the jungle.

We were lifted off the ground and gaining height as I spoke. "I've only heard hunters mentioned once before today, so I really have no clue who you guys are, let alone who a commanding officer would be. But if you're talking about the grungy musician, David Ward, then yes I know him but I can't picture him out on some killing spree."

"Ward has always been excellent at discretion."

I closed my eyes to breathe as my ears began to pop from the elevation. "If Dave knows that I'm with you then Julius told him to look out for me." I sighed and opened my eyes to look for gum in my backpack. "I told you that my story is complicated and I'm not sure how much I want to share right now."

"And Julius is?" He tried to probe me for more info as he held out a stick of gum.

"Julius…was a friend…until Maxx found him. He made a deal to save me and today in the jungle was the first time I've seen him since then." *Technically true, if you didn't count the dreams.*

"He was the hybrid with Maxx? This was the first we've seen of him. We didn't know what or who he was, but he's just as fucking vicious as Maxx."

I turned away from him and looked at the night sky outside my window. It was my fault Julius was even in this mess. I knew he was still a good man, especially if he had sought out Dave to check on me.

The plane finally stabilized and after a moment Calvin held a blanket out toward me. "Get some sleep, we'll be in Wichita in about five hours."

Wichita… I was going back to the Midwest. I pulled the blanket into my lap not bothering to unfold it. I wasn't cold but I was tired.

I didn't want to sleep though, that much I knew. The last thing I needed was to have another dream involving Maxx or Julius. I stared out the window instead and tried to count the city lights until there was nothing but darkness.

I must have fallen back asleep because I was sitting in an arm chair facing an elaborate fireplace. There was no other light but for the dancing flames as I took in my surroundings. There was an identical chair to mine just to the right of me, a half drank glass of something atop a table between the chairs.

Maxx could be seen outlined by shadows as he sat staring into the fire. "How often does this happen, Miss Donovan? I can imagine you are not very fond of seeing me so frequently."

I was surprised that he was speaking to me, but based on the timing I assumed it wasn't completely chance that I was here.

"Almost every time I sleep."

"Before or after our last meeting?"

"After."

He continued to stare into the fire, "You have somehow been able to mask your presence then. I very seldom had knowledge that you were there."

"I turn and walk away every time it happens. I don't want to be there but I don't know how else to make it stop. The further away I get the quicker I wake back up."

He reached over and picked up his beverage. "The hunters can help you. They'll expect your loyalty in return of course."

He stood with his glass in hand, still not looking my direction as he started to walk to the exit somewhere behind me. "I need you to tell Hobbes that you're a dream walker, he can make them *stop."*

"Hobbes?"   Usually when I questioned anything I didn't get any answers.

"The bald one, Calvin Richard Hobbes, he may be named after a cartoon but he is excellent at what he does.   Why do you think I always let him live?"

His steps stopped and then grew closer once again until his hot breath pressed against my ear. I could smell the trace of whisky as he whispered to me, "You need to stay away from Julius, Miss Donovan.   Remember the deal."

I bolted awake and sat gasping for breath as I looked to see that I was still on the plane.   I could still smell the whiskey as I tried to calm myself down.

Most of the other men were all asleep except for Calvin who was watching me suspiciously from across the aisle.

I stretched my legs as I stood and walked to the small bathroom stall to splash water on my face. I looked at myself in the mirror and wondered if I really wanted to tell the hunters about my dreams. Could they really make them stop?

I had somewhat cleaned myself up back at the base but my hair was still tangled.   It was almost long enough to brush my shoulders, but I knew I would cut it the first chance I got.   I untied a piece of twine from my wrist and used it to pull my hair up into a makeshift bun before opening the door to go back out.

Calvin was standing there waiting. I took a moment to study him before I moved. He was maybe an inch taller than myself, just clearing six feet in height, but it was all the bulky muscle that made him appear larger. His biceps bulged from beneath his tight black t-shirt and my eyes wandered down his arms as I admired all the tattoo work.

Even though he shaved his head bald it was more for convenience because he didn't look a day over 30, maybe 35 at the very most. His eyes were tired though, as if life hadn't been kind to him at all.

His blue eyes stared into mine and I finally dropped my gaze and stepped aside.

"Are you okay?" He hadn't made a move towards the bathroom and I knew that he was somewhat worried about me.

"Just a nightmare." My voice was a bare whisper as I strayed in the cramped hall.

"Those happen often?"

"More than I'd like." I glanced at the sleeping men and didn't want to risk waking any of them. He must have seen my glance because he squeezed past me and waved me to follow to the rear of the plane.

There was a door that opened to a meeting room with a large table surrounded by chairs. He closed the door behind me and went to a cabinet as I chose a seat near the table's head.

He handed me a bottle of water before taking the seat across from me. We sat in silence awhile as I wondered where to start before he stood to pull off his shirt.

"Start here," he said pointing to an ugly scar on his shoulder. "How were you there the day Maxx destroyed my shoulder?"

"You were shot in the chest too, I don't see any scars there." The original dream passed through my mind as I recalled seeing him collapse to the ground after taking several shots to the chest.

"I was wearing a vest, I had some serious bruising but no actual wounds."

I looked at the various scars across his arms and shivered. "I was asleep... I thought it had been just a nightmare but when I woke up Maxx was in my house... It was the first time I had ever seen either of you."

I closed my eyes to compose myself as my hands fumbled around the water bottle. "He grabbed hold of my arm leaving some kind of tattoo and told me he needed me to find someone but then he left without telling me anymore.

"I met Julius almost the same day but it wasn't until months later that he actually touched the tattoo and it flared with pain. I went home, but Maxx was there waiting and took me with him when I refused to hand over Julius."

My words broke and I took another breath to try and make it through, "I was tortured a few days before I woke up safe back home. Julius said he made a deal to save me as long as I would stay away from him."

Calvin had already put his shirt back on and sat back down as I continued on. "So, I called some friends and came to the jungle to move on and get my mind onto other things.   But the nightmares started again and I would see Maxx again wherever he was.   I would try to turn and walk away to wake myself up, but tonight I recognized where he was. I started to run and then plowed into you.

"It must have been the key to wake me up because I was back at camp then."

"That would explain the teleportation stunt you pulled.   Why did you come back after you woke up?"

"You were alive, and as much as I wanted to deny everything I had been through, I knew I wouldn't be able to unless I ran back and saw it myself while awake.   I knew it was real."

"What about the nightmare you had just a bit ago?   Was that Maxx again?"

I nodded.   "He realized that I've been able to see him so he wanted to put an end to it.   He said I should tell you that I'm a dream walker and you would be able to help me."

"How considerate of him, anything else?"

"He told me to stay away from Julius."

He leaned back and drank his water. "Dream walkers don't usually have the ability to manifest their physical form when they travel, especially untrained ones."

"I don't understand it but I need it to stop." I tried to keep my voice even but I could hear the shakiness just below the surface.

"You must have some kind of majik background or bloodline.   Either of your parents' supes?"

"My mother killed herself when I was 17 and I never had any knowledge of my father." There was no emotion in my voice as I confessed what I hoped would drop the topic. "What are hunters?"

"We try and protect Earth realm from any rebellious species. Earth prides itself on being a neutral ground and any non-human that lives here is to not bring attention to themselves or discuss the details of other realms without valid reason. Granted, most of Earth's population is made up of ordinary non-majik humans, but there are quite a few different species that reside here as well.

"For each species there is typically another realm out there. I know we haven't learned them all yet, but here's at least a half dozen we know of that are similar to earth but so very different as well. A lot of these other realms don't get along and during wars or even simple power struggles between ruling families a few criminals will come to earth realm for an escape or for the purpose of banishment.

"We welcome them, but only if they agree to our terms and are able to blend into human society. Demons are the only species that seem unable to follow such a rule. They may blend in at first glance but their love of fire and chaos makes settling here difficult."

The plane took a violent shake and Calvin stopped his explanation to go look out the window. A flash of lightning crossed the sky before he was able to pull the shade back down.

"Hunters have been around for a very long time. We are typically made up of different supernatural species that were born and raised here on earth. Occasionally we will run into a majik wielding human that got mixed up with the wrong crowd and want a way to keep it from happening again."

"People like me?" I knew what he was implying. Maxx had shown up in my life and caused complete chaos by changing everything about my world views. I hated him for it and didn't want to ever feel so vulnerable again.

"Yes, people like you. People that choose to arm themselves with knowledge and power instead of denying the truth that has been thrown directly into their face."

I thought about it and realized he was right. I wouldn't be able to move on with life by trying to ignore what had happened. I had spent weeks in the jungle with friends attempting to forget, but it still followed me.

There wasn't much of a decision to make anymore but I knew without a doubt I would join the hunters. I didn't look forward to seeing Julius of Maxx again anytime soon, but I knew it would happen eventually and I would hopefully be prepared by then.

"What do I need to do?"

A smile crept across Calvin's face as if he had known my choice all along. "Well, you already got on my plane, so you're off to a good start. When we get to base we can match you with a witch to see what majik you have and get the dream walking under control."

"And after that?"

"Combat, physical, and weapons training... Intensive majik training as well as hitting the books and learning about all the other species. It's just the basic stuff, but the whole thing can be pretty intense."

"Right." It sounded like military training camp and I wondered how well I would do. "How long does it usually take?"

"Typically twelve weeks for the basic training and then a month or so of local patrols before being able to join longer distance hunts."

I nodded, "That doesn't sound too difficult."

He laughed, "No darlin' not at all." I could hear the sarcasm dripping from the words.

"I'll be joining hunts by April." My voice was deadpan serious and his laughter stopped.

"Most recruits take almost six full months to get to that point, the only exception being those with prior military training."

"I'm a quick study."

"We'll see."

The pilot came over the intercom then, "We're approaching the destination, please prepare for landing."

I reached down and buckled my seatbelt, not having to leave the table. "Is your name really Calvin Hobbes?"

His head shot up at my question and the

laughter must have shown on my face because his smile made an appearance again.

"Yeah, my parents thought they were clever."

Chapter Fourteen

Three weeks later I was sore in every part of my body. I hadn't exactly let myself go the last few years I had been playing house, but I wasn't exactly used to a lot of physical activity anymore.

I had a weekend off before training began to head back to Kansas City to gather clothes and personal items from my house. I let curiosity get the best of me and drove past the area Julius lived only to see his house gone and only rubble remaining. It proved to me that I needed to move on and throw myself completely into the training, so I did.

Early mornings were spent doing physical activities, running a few miles, making it through obstacle course, and weight training. Sometimes it would alternate, but it was almost the same thing daily.

By 9 am I was in a classroom setting learning about different species of people from other worlds. All my life I had only known about earth and toyed with the idea of life on other planets, but I had never imagined my sci-fi thinking would actually be right.

Lunch would be around noon followed by

majik lessons.   I was a natural so far and it was determined that I had to have come from a powerful bloodline.

Evenings involved another physical training session but on a lighter regime than the morning routine.

At eight weeks I had become used to the training and pushed myself even harder than the others.   I was excelling at majik, able to cast spells and use them in the blink of an eye.   Teleportation was still a tricky task but I almost had it down.

By ten weeks I had surpassed all others and was lined up to start joining local patrols.   True to my word I had managed to get it done before March had ended and spent the next two weeks on uneventful, yet successful patrols.

Dave showed up to congratulate me on completing the program.   He didn't say much else since we had never really been close friends, regardless it was nice seeing a familiar face.

The hunter networks hadn't found a single trace of Maxx over the past few months, and it wasn't unusual for him to vanish and spend time on other realms.

While others busied themselves with larger problems I was sent to Dallas with a couple guys. There had been some demon activity in the area, but nothing to signify more than a couple of them.

We were in the Deep Ellum district on a Thursday night when we found our targets.   Two male and a female leaving the tall black brick building that was a well-known night club.

I hesitated at first, my senses saying demon but they didn't seem to be doing anything wrong. My hesitation almost cost me as one spun around conjuring fire and throwing it at me. I managed to knock it away with my own majik but they were already running.

My other teammate was waiting a few blocks up the road and stepped out in time to block their way. One of the males didn't stop in time and found the wrong end of Nate's blade as his head tumbled to the ground. I had my gun out before the female turned back my way, her eyes flashing red as she summoned majik to throw at me.

I summoned my own as I pulled the trigger and sent the bullets and majik flying together. Her chest exploded outward at the hit and she fell to the ground.

The third demon had run back past me towards the club with Nathan in hot pursuit. I started to chase them but they had quite the lead. I had lost focus on my surroundings and a fourth demon knocked me to the ground as I passed the club.

I rolled into the fall, jumping back up just as quick to fight back. Before I could even throw a punch his neck snapped and flames consumed his body.

I hadn't been the one to use majik so my head shot up as I scanned the area.

Julius was standing at the door of the club

watching me.   I froze as my eyes locked on his, but just as quickly he vanished.

Nathan came jogging back up the street in time to see me standing by the burning corpse.

"You get points for theatrics but we gotta get this cleaned up and get out of here.   I'll get the truck."   He took off at a jog again leaving me alone in the street as the heavy bass of the club drowned out the silence ringing in my ears.

My hand shook as I held it out towards the burning demon.   I absorbed the majik to put out the flames and a smooth warmth spread through me.

All majik left a trace of its user, everyone having their own unique feel.   As the warmth spread through me, I could feel the signature of Julius and I knew I would remember that distinct feeling forever.

The truck came rumbling up the street and Nathan jumped out to help me lift the body and throw it into the back.   We got the other three and went back to the hotel to meet our other teammate.

The next few hunts and patrols all went about the same way but I didn't always see Julius. The bigger cities where activity was highest were the places I swore I caught glimpses of him. During fights I would finish the kill and see him from the corner of my eye.

Smaller hunts for other species were less exciting, but holy shit, teleportation came in handy when you were trying to chase a rogue wolf or vamp.

No one else ever noticed Julius, and he had managed to stay off the radar enough that none of the hunters would even recognize him even if they saw him.

So when he walked into a bar that a group of us were celebrating in, no one gave him a second glance.   He took a seat at the bar and ordered a drink while pay attention to some sports game on the television.   A few times he looked my way and smiled at me, having the bartender bring me a couple shots of vodka with 'meet me outside' written on the napkin.

I shoved the napkin in my pocket and kept a smile on my face as the group continued to laugh and drink as I watched Julius walk out the door.

I made a trip to the bathroom before announcing my exit.   "I'm calling it a night gentlemen, I need my beauty sleep you know!"   I patted my face for dramatic effect and they all laughed and demanded I have one more drink before I left.   I obliged with another shot of vodka before making it out the door to the noisy Atlanta streets.

Julius was leaned up against the front of the building waiting for me.   He didn't utter a word as he turned and led us to a nearby hotel.   I silently followed him as he pulled a key from his pocket and held a room door open for me to enter.

"You could have just called."   I joked as he pushed the door shut.

"We keep ending up in the same place anyway, I figured this was easier."   His words were clipped and harsh but my knees still went weak at the sound of his voice. "You couldn't just leave it alone and stay away? I made a deal so you could go back to your life and be safe."

"I tried that, but my life took me to the same jungle as you." The hallway felt too small for the both of us as I took a step backward and ended up flush against the wall.

Memories surged to the surface as I stood inches away staring up into his eyes. He must have felt them as well because he stepped back and paced the hall.

He was more dangerous than ever, deadly to me but it didn't stop my hormones from raging. I wanted him again just as much as the first time I had met him and I wanted the raw primal energy that coursed between us.

"I realized in the jungle that I had some kind of majik in my blood Julius. At least with the hunters I can use the power I have. I had to either ignore the truth or embrace it and use it for something good."

His pacing stopped and he stalked over to me, his body pinning mine as his hands landed flat on the wall on either side of my head. "What exactly is good about this? Out chasing danger? This is not good for you, *I am not good for you*. I can't keep trying to protect you from myself when you show up in my life at every turn."

He still couldn't look into my eyes while he spoke and I knew I had to get his attention somehow. "I don't need your protection Julius."

My majik flashed out at him to back my words and that was all it took.

His gaze locked onto mine moments before his mouth claimed my own and I was lost mind body and soul.   Our majik danced back and forth between us, the power magnifying with each hot breath we exchanged.   We were no longer in the filthy hotel room and I wondered which of us did the teleportation.

Chapter Fifteen

*** Jacki ***

Thinking I was asleep, he pressed a gentle kiss to my temple later that night before he slipped out to take care of some business.   I would be going back to Haelexii with him later in the day. In that moment I knew that his deal was broken and mine was finished.   There would be nothing keeping us apart and neither of us even knew how lost we both were.

As I lay alone in his bed my hand went to the hemp necklace at my throat.   My fingers toyed with the crystal as I thought about my last visit to Hael Realm.

"I had a visitor shortly after I marked you, Miss Donovan."   Maxx's voice filled the room as I regained consciousness.   I looked around confused and remembered being taken from my home.   He said he was going to take me to the demon realm, but this didn't seem like hell.

All the lore spoke of a fiery pit but I was in a plush bed in a luxurious air conditioned room.

"Your father seemed less than pleased that you were being visited by demons.   I of course, had no idea whom he meant and you can imagine my surprise when I learned that YOU were the bastard child of the infamous Grant DeCartanion. Even though you had no knowledge about your heritage, your natural majik ability made sense."

I blinked a few times at his pacing around before he started talking again. "He insisted I remove my mark from you and since I knew you had already accomplished your task I toyed with the idea of complying with him."

He took a seat in a reclining chair next to my bed and I sat up to face him. "So I told your daddy dearest that I would back away from you, but I started to think about the potential of power that would come from a union between our bastard children. ...and well, now I have a proposition for you." He leaned closer and smiled, "It seems that my bleeding heart of a son is quite fond of you. I can almost guarantee that he is going to bargain for your safety and he is going to want you away from this life to live a nice happy human existence...

"You're going to play along. You're going to play up the tortured and broken role and stay away from him for a while. After some time I'm sure you'll find the hunters and join them. You'll learn to hunt and the potential that your own blood contains. All the while, I will have my son here with me. When I think you are both ready I will ensure that you meet again on a few hunts and I don't want you to hold back. I want you to fight and prove that you aren't weak.

"He will feel your power and you will win

him over. He will think you are better off at his side than across enemy lines. You will be his bride and he will never know that it was the plan from the beginning."

It was ludicrous, "And if I say no? If I stay away from the hunters and don't take your goddamn deals?" I met his gaze and held firm.

"If she says no..." he paused for his standard dramatic effect, "Grant, would you care to explain to her why she can't walk away from this?"

My father walked into the room.

I had only seen him once before and it had been ten years ago, but he still looked exactly the same. "The majik is in your blood and now that you've left earth realm, you won't be able to suppress that power and pass for human. You will be a target for every demon and power thirsty creature that exists on earth. I can only help you if you agree to his terms."

Maxx seemed delighted to chime in, "my demons will find you and you will have no choice but to fight them or die. It will be so much easier on you to simply follow through and attack them first, as a hunter." His smile grew wider, "it really is simple Miss Donovan. Be yourself and allow this attraction to flourish in the way nature wishes."

"How am I supposed to do this if I can't pass for human any longer?" It was a simple question that they were expecting.

"Your father is very skilled at majik and the art of masking one's true identity. So long as you keep your end of the deal, the majik will remain."

My father stepped closer to me, opening his hand to reveal a necklace made of hemp rope like the one I had always worn in the past. "May I?" He asked as he stopped at the foot of the bed and gestured toward my neck. I nodded and he stepped forward, fastening it in one quick movement.

He leaned away and looked into my eyes a moment as I watched so many emotions cross his face before he turned back away.

Maxx clapped his hands in delight. "That settles it, do we have a deal then Miss Donovan?"

My fingers traced the twine around my throat and wrapped around the lone white crystal hanging down from it. A single tear slid down my cheek as I nodded.

I used to wish there was more to life than the everyday eat sleep work repeat, but now I knew better. Everything I once knew had changed. The world wasn't as simple as humans thought. There were monsters and evil far beyond their darkest nightmares and it was only the beginning.

I had served my time in hell and I signed my own contract to get out. I made a deal with the devil and all he wanted in return was for me to fully conquer his son. I was a witch who hunted demons but I was married to their Prince. By joining with Julius my contract was fulfilled and I only hoped that he never found out about my betrayal.

To be continued…

A NOTE FROM THE AUTHOR

Okay, so I know the 'to be continued' bit is cruel, but I had to do it!

Seriously, I have to give you something to look forward to, and who's to say that the next thing you read will even be about Jacki or Julius?

So what do you think? Was Jacki working for Maxx the whole time? Who exactly is her father? How pissed is Julius going to be if/when he finds out? What about the hunters?

I'm sure there are a lot more questions, but that's okay, send them to me if you want, but I may never answer you.
Or maybe I will….

You never know. :)

ACKNOWLEDGEMENTS

A BIG big thanks to my beta team!
You guys don't even know how awesome you are!
I appreciate you more than you can ever know and
I'm so glad to have such a great team of friends that
were able to help me in this journey.
Cat Nordstrom, Clara Short, Georgia Carter, Joell
Brock, Kelli Thompson, Kirsty Fitzpatrick, Renay
Huff, Sarah Ward, and Shauna Sarver.
You lot are my dream team!

A very special thanks to Fayce for the late night
texts and snapchats to keep me going.   Thank you
for letting me bounce ideas off of you and for
cracking the whip to make sure I finished this.
We've always dreamed big, and let this be a
reminder to both of us that we should never-ever
give up on those dreams no matter how big or small
they may be.   I love you.

ABOUT THE AUTHOR

 Jezka is one of those women that grabbed life by the barbed wire, jumped the fence, and kept running into the distance. She has hitchhiked across the United States for fun, and will stubbornly go out of her way to prove people wrong when told "you can't do that!"

She has always had a passion for writing, but the attention span of a goldfish, so sometimes it took a while to actually get a story told.

She loves adventure, but lately has taken to being "responsible" and taking some college classes in an effort to focus on her health.

She currently lives in South-Central Kansas with her Chucky Doll.

Find Jezka online!!!

http://www.JezkaBrash.com

http://www.amazon.com

https://www.goodreads.com/Aneikiodos

http://www.facebook.com/JezkaBrashAuthor

Curious about the mark constantly mentioned in this book?   It's on the cover!

But I figured I'd include it here as well for some of you that want to see the whole thing.

Special thanks go out to Sarah R. Ward for helping me get this design on paper before I had any sort of photo editing skills.   I'm glad to have this image on my skin as a permanent reminder of not only our demons, but our friendship.

Made in the USA
Middletown, DE
26 July 2017